"You're li[ke] ... [fi]lled with raw excitement," Spencer said softly

"Does that line work very often?" Brenna asked.

He wanted to laugh at her ability to read him so clearly. "I don't know. I've never used it before." The bed pushed their bodies closer together. She bumped gently against him. The motion was sensual, sexual, arousing. "I think you'd better tell me to stop," Spencer warned.

Brenna looked up at him, her lips parted, her eyes filled with need. That was all the incentive he needed. "Too late." He covered her lips, teasing her, tasting her. Suddenly he couldn't get enough. His hands slid beneath her sweatshirt to stroke her silken body, to explore the lissome length of her. Lightning split the sky. The room rocked beneath a new blast of thunder. The bed rocked with it.

He'd never felt so hot, so out of control. Her body writhed beneath his touch. The waterbed writhed, as well.

"You're driving me crazy," Spencer whispered as his hand slid across the plane of her stomach, under her panties, finding the dampness that waited there.

Brenna curved upward, straining toward his touch. "Yes!"

The bed rolled. Water, cold and wet, soaked his shoulder. "Oh, no..." Spencer groaned. "We've sprung a leak!"

Creating lighthearted, sexy stories for Harlequin Temptation is something **Dani Sinclair** has wanted to do for years. And the characters in *The Naked Truth* must have known it. They sprang to life in her computer one day and promptly set about having wicked fun in a bid to have their story told.

An avid reader, Dani has written stories ever since she can remember. Not until her sister asked her to write a romance did Dani begin to take her own writing seriously. That first, unpolished attempt told her she'd found her niche. With full support of her husband of thirty years and their two grown sons, she plans to continue to fill that niche with more stories of love, laughter and romance. Dani also enjoys writing action-packed romantic suspense for Harlequin Intrigue.

Books by Dani Sinclair

HARLEQUIN INTRIGUE
371—MYSTERY BABY
401—MAN WITHOUT A BADGE
448—BETTER WATCH OUT

THE NAKED TRUTH
Dani Sinclair

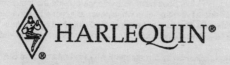

TORONTO • NEW YORK • LONDON
AMSTERDAM • PARIS • SYDNEY • HAMBURG
STOCKHOLM • ATHENS • TOKYO • MILAN • MADRID
PRAGUE • WARSAW • BUDAPEST • AUCKLAND

This book is lovingly dedicated to my sister,
Barbara Ann Hein, who always believed in me, and to
Brenda Chin and Bonnie Crisalli, who gave me the
opportunities to fulfill my dreams.

Friendship and many thanks go to Robyn Amos,
Mary McGowan, Barbie Richardson and Vicki Singer,
who gave unstinting support.

ISBN 0-373-25790-2

THE NAKED TRUTH

Copyright © 1998 by Patricia A. Gagne.

Printed in U.S.A.

1

His GRANDMOTHER was going to get him killed—or ten to twenty in a state penitentiary. Why the devil had he let her talk him into this?

Spencer Griffen eyed the massive maple tree to the side of the house with distaste. He lifted the ridiculous ski mask from his face and allowed the soft night breeze to cool his skin. Inside the dark leather gloves, his hands were sweating, but he left the gloves on. His fingers were used to gripping pencils, not tree bark.

Resigned, he swung his body onto the lowest branch, glad he still played enough sports to keep himself fit. The last time he'd climbed a tree, he'd been ten years old. When he got stuck, his baby-sitter had panicked and called the fire department.

He wondered what a fireman would say this time.

Spencer grimaced as he moved steadily upward until he was level with the second-story balcony. The thick limb dangling over the balcony supported his weight as he swung himself out and over, but he landed with more noise than he'd expected. He crouched, hardly daring to breathe, and waited. No one came running to investigate.

Quickly he pulled the mask back down to cover his face and moved to the sliding glass door. He prayed his grandmother was right and there were no alarms on the second floor. If not, he was in for a sudden career change—making license plates.

From the tool pouch at his waist, he drew out the

fancy glass cutter and suction cup. Somewhat to his surprise, the device worked. Minutes later he slipped inside the darkened room. He closed the door and adjusted the drapes, set the cut piece of glass on a tabletop, replaced the tools, and removed a flashlight from his belt.

His grandmother called Hadden Caldwell Summerton Sr. an art collector. Flashing the beam of light around the room, Spencer decided Hadden Senior also had been a dirty old man. Spencer frowned as he studied the nearest oil painting, a little shocked by the graphic display of erotica.

His grandmother, the minister's wife, had seen this? Not while his grandfather was alive, he'd wager.

Twelve paintings hung in the sitting room. Three depicted single subjects. He gave those pictures close attention, but there was only one reclining nude, and it wasn't exactly in a classic pose.

Spencer bit back an expletive.

"Someone had quite an imagination," he muttered under his breath.

He turned and surveyed the other walls before stepping through the connecting door into the bedroom itself. His scalp began to tingle, bringing him to an immediate halt. He was being watched.

The flashlight beam played about the room. A full-sized armor-suited knight nearly gave him heart failure before he realized it wasn't a living person.

A suit of armor in a bedroom filled with pornographic artwork? Spencer didn't even want to know why.

He tried to ignore the prickle of his skin and the pounding of his heart, but the sensation of being watched persisted. Hadden's grandson and heir, Hadden Caldwell Summerton III, should be out at a dinner party with his brand-new fiancée. Only the live-in cook-housekeeper and her husband were supposed to be on the premises right now. Spencer found it highly doubtful that either of them was hiding in the old man's bedroom—unless they had come in here to be titillated by the artwork. He had to admit some of these paintings were…interesting.

The flashlight steadied on the open door to the bathroom and a closed door he assumed led to a closet. Fighting an urge to turn around and go back out the way he'd come, Spencer crossed the room, took a deep breath, and flung open the closet. His fingers found the wall switch and the enclosure bloomed with light. Neatly organized rows of suits, jackets, pants and shirts stretched before him.

He switched off the light, shut the closet door and, taking another deep breath, entered the bathroom.

"Good grief."

Lights over the dual sinks illuminated a room that could only be called a sybarite's delight. In the center of the room, the enormous bathtub roosted on a thickly carpeted pedestal of white. It could easily seat three. Ferns and other plants added color, perched on the heads or hands of nude female statuary scattered behind the tub.

Spencer moved further into the room and decided Hadden had probably held some interesting parties in the massive shower stall—empty at the moment. The commode had its own private alcove, tucked neatly out of sight. Mirrors filled most of the bathroom wall space, but there were spots for a few more paintings. He scanned them quickly. Highly erotic paintings at that.

"Hedonistic old geezer," he muttered.

Hadden Summerton Sr. might have been seventy-eight years old when he died, but he clearly had the mind of a randy teenager. Spencer backed up and bumped against a freestanding statue near the door. He caught it before it toppled, then blinked as he realized what he held. Quickly, he released the plaster breast and buttock. Beautifully sculpted, and more than a little pornographic, the figures were forever frozen with expressions of almost painful delight—particularly the man in the middle.

Spencer shook his head. His social life was far from dull, but it had been several months since he'd done more than kiss a woman. This stuff was starting to get to him. He needed to find his grandmother's painting and get the heck out of here.

The barest trace of noise from the bedroom sent him spinning around, flashlight raised like a club. As his eyes readjusted to the darkness, he realized a long shadowy figure was attempting to inch its way from beneath the king-sized bed.

With a curse, he hurled himself forward.

There was a muffled squeak of surprise. Then he found himself trying to hold a writhing, bucking tangle of arms and legs. They rolled across the carpeting until his hand suddenly landed on something distinctly soft and round where there should have been a rock-hard chest wall.

He stopped moving. So did she.

"A woman?" he asked.

From a spot on the floor a few inches away, his fallen flashlight beam illuminated them. Long strands of dark hair covered part of a decidedly feminine face.

"Very astute, buster. Now, move that hand or I'm going to turn you into a eunuch," she spat at him.

Spencer instantly moved his hand from the firm breast it cupped to a womanly length of upper arm covered by dark material. Considering her position, he found himself wryly amused by her courage.

"Uh, don't take this wrong, but I don't think you're in any position to dictate terms," he told her.

Instantly, she proved him wrong.

With one thrust of her knee, she nearly kept her promise. He barely managed to keep her pinned beneath him.

"Damn. That hurt," he muttered.

"Good," she said fiercely. "Now, get off me."

Her face lay in shadow, turned away from the flashlight, but she didn't sound the least bit intimidated by her current position.

"I don't think so," he panted. "Who are you and what are you doing in here?"

"I could ask you the same thing. You weigh a ton. Let me up."

Yeah, and the minute he did, she'd scream bloody murder. She squirmed beneath him, reminding him just how long he'd been celibate.

"Will you lie still?"

"No." Her eyes glittered in the dark.

The lady had guts. She was also, unexpectedly, turning him on. She smelled clean and fresh and womanly and she was soft in all the right places.

"Look, I don't want to hurt you—"

"Then get up!"

This time, he recognized a core of fear in her voice. With him sprawled on top of her like this, she probably thought the next thing he'd do was try to rape her, he realized. And no wonder. Immediately, he let her go and rolled away, embarrassed by his body's betrayal.

She scrambled back and upward, bumping against the massive wood chest of drawers. Her position was defensive but determined as she faced him.

"I'm not going to hurt you," he told her quietly.

"Right." Her voice shook slightly.

"Really. Just take it easy. Who the hell are you?"

Her chin lifted in defiance. "Wouldn't you like to know?"

"Yes, actually, I would. No one is supposed to be in the house except the cook and her husband, and you can't be the cook."

"Why not?"

"Because she's German."

"*Sprechen Sie Deutsch?*" she asked sweetly, getting to her feet warily.

He followed suit, prepared to lunge for her if she started to scream. "Your accent is terrible."

"Yeah? Well, my English is just fine, so suppose you tell me what you're doing up here? The silver's downstairs."

He straightened his glasses beneath the ski mask and smiled. "How do you know that?"

"I'm the cook, remember?"

He watched her features set in mutinous lines and bent to recover the flashlight. "So you say."

Light abruptly crept beneath the door leading to the hall.

"Damn," he muttered. Someone had decided to investigate the noise.

Spencer lunged forward and grabbed her before she could shout a warning. No time to get to the balcony, assuming he could drag her that far, but the bathroom door was still open behind him.

"Not a sound," he hissed in her ear, tugging her through the doorway. Amazingly, she didn't resist. In fact, she seemed almost as eager to get inside as he was. No sooner had he closed the door than he heard the bedroom door open.

Reciting a litany of inventive curses in his head, Spencer realized this was the end of the line. One squeak from her and life as he'd known it would come to a most unpleasant end.

He tugged her unresisting body backward toward the isolated commode stall where he straddled the bowl and pulled her tightly against his body so they wouldn't be seen right away. Belatedly, he realized he'd positioned her like a shield, and one hand cupped her left breast. Too late to change now, but he prayed the person investigating wasn't armed or trigger-happy. Spencer held her against his chest, afraid to breathe.

The bathroom door opened and light cascaded through the room. Seconds passed like eons before the light went out, plunging them back into utter darkness. The bathroom door closed with a loud click.

Abruptly, the woman began to wriggle her head to and fro.

Spencer tried to grip her more tightly, but the flashlight in his gloved hand made it almost impossible to hold her still and maintain his precarious stance. She finally twisted her head to one side and bit down hard. The soft leather of the glove saved his skin, but the bite still hurt.

"Damn."

"Can't breathe," she gasped in a tiny whisper before he could get his hand back over her mouth.

Spencer hesitated. She hadn't screamed, and she stopped struggling as soon as she got her mouth uncovered. They both heard the bedroom door snap shut.

"Why didn't you call for help?" he whispered in her ear. The fragrantly clean scent that kept tantalizing him seemed to emanate from her long dark hair where it brushed against his face. He realized his grip had shifted so his arm now crossed over both her breasts. He wondered if she was wearing a bra.

"Because I didn't have enough oxygen, you big oaf," she whispered right back.

"You do now," he pointed out, very much aware that her nipples were growing rigid beneath his arm.

"So I do." She took a deep breath and he clamped his hand back over her mouth. She promptly kicked him in the shin, nearly knocking him into the open commode. Spencer lost his hold completely in his effort to stay out of the toilet bowl.

She tore free and whirled around. "Will you be quiet?" she groused. "Do you want him to come back?"

That startled him into immobility. "You don't want to be rescued?"

"I don't need to be rescued."

She had a point. One good shove and all she'd have to do was flush. He wondered if she knew his grandmother. That sweet old lady could lay a man flat with a look. The two of them had a lot in common.

"I don't want you pulling a gun and shooting anyone," she warned him.

His grandmother would have added a wagging finger in his face. Then again, maybe this woman had too. All he could see was her outline. Spencer flicked on the flashlight.

"I don't have a gun," he admitted.

She muttered something under her breath.

"Hey, I heard that. I may be inept, but I am not an idiot." Well, not certifiable, anyhow.

Until tonight.

"I don't believe this," she muttered more loudly.

"Me either. Are you going to call for help?" he asked.

"Eventually."

"Eventually?" Flummoxed, he stepped out of the narrow enclosure to face her.

She was tall, he realized, five ten or so. No wonder he'd taken her for a man when he'd only glimpsed her outline on the floor. But no one who ever saw her face would make that mistake.

"What are you doing here?" she demanded.

"What does it look like I'm doing here?" He was stung into responding. He moved to come between her and the door. His fingers sought and found the light switch. They both blinked in the sudden glare.

"Looks to me like you're bungling a burglary attempt," she told him.

"Bungling.... Who the hell are you?" he demanded. Now that his eyes were adjusting, he realized she wore tight black pants and a baggy black sweatshirt. Thanks to his unexpected groping, he could make a pretty good guess at what the sweatshirt concealed.

Atop her long regal neck sat an oval face with high cheekbones and wide blue eyes, a classical face that would age with style and beauty. She brushed self-consciously at her long dark hair where it had come unbound from some sort of twist in the back.

"Cute mask," she sniped.

Automatically, he straightened the thing, since it tended to slip away from one eye.

"Glad you like it." He ran his eyes over her attire once more. "Since you didn't call for help, can I assume you broke in here too?"

She looked away. "Of course not. I walked in. Trust me, it beats the heck out of climbing trees. Though I must say, that trick with the glass cutter is pretty nifty. I've never seen that done except on television."

"Who says there's nothing educational on television anymore?" he asked.

"Look, if I help you, will you promise to leave and not hurt me?"

"I have no intention of hurting you." He shook his head in disbelief. "You're going to help me?"

"I will if it will get you out of here quickly. I'm sure Hadden is insured, and he'll be back anytime now," she added.

"You're going to help a burglar?"

She planted her hands on her hips and glared at him. "I'm going to do whatever is necessary to make you leave before someone gets hurt."

Spencer rubbed at his chin through the ski mask, wishing he could rub the places where she'd kicked him as well. "The only one who seems to be getting hurt around here is me, but don't worry."

"I won't."

"I meant, don't worry, because we have plenty of time," he said dryly. "Hadden won't be back for a while. He went to dinner with his fiancée."

"No, he didn't."

Her chest rose and fell in exasperation beneath the sweatshirt. It was a very nice chest, he decided.

She crossed her arms over her breasts as if she'd heard his thoughts.

"I saw him leave," Spencer informed her.

"Maybe so, but dinner got canceled at the last minute."

"And you know this because you're the cook?"

For just a second she appeared startled, then she nodded. "Of course, and I have to get back downstairs and finish cleaning the kitchen."

"Now why do I have a hard time believing that?" More than likely, she planned to finish taking whatever she had come to steal, but this was probably not the best time to argue with her.

"I'm sure it has something to do with your intelligence quotient," she said sweetly.

"Lady, don't you know it isn't wise to bait a fellow burglar?"

"*I* am not a burglar." Color stained her cheekbones.

"Uh-huh. Look, if Hadden didn't go to dinner, I don't suppose you know where he did go?"

"Yes, as a matter of fact. He's dropping something by a friend's house. That won't take long, so we have to hurry."

"We. As in you and me?"

"I want you out of here."

Her haughty demeanor amazed him. "How do you know where he went?"

"What difference does it make? We're running out of time."

"Oh, hell." It suddenly dawned on him who she had to be. "You're the fiancée, aren't you? What's your name? Kelsey? Kerry? Yeah. Kerry. Kerry Martin."

He should have realized it immediately. Her assured attitude, her presence in the house... Only, how come she wasn't hollering blue murder? Or at least scared to death. As far as she knew, he was a real burglar.

She straightened her shoulders and glared at him. "Who I am doesn't matter."

"I assume it does to Hadden."

She flattened her hands on her hips drawing his attention to their nicely rounded curves even as she managed to glare regally. "Look, do you know how to get inside the safe or not?"

"You want me to break into a safe for you?"

"Not for me," she said quickly. "I assume that's what you're here for."

"I hate to disillusion you, but I didn't even know Hadden had a safe."

"Well, he does. Come on. And try to keep quiet. We don't want Alvin coming back up here."

Alvin, he knew, was the cook's husband and general handyman. "You're right. We don't want him coming back up here. Unless maybe he'd like to help us too?"

"Very funny."

She came toward him with arrogant grace. Before he knew what she intended, she plucked the flashlight from his hand and pushed past him, allowing him another whiff of that tantalizing fragrance.

"Turn off the light," she commanded over her shoulder.

Spencer obeyed, amused again despite himself.

"Want to tell me why you were hiding under the bed?" he asked.

"No."

He chuckled. If she wasn't going to turn him in, it might be interesting to see what she wanted from the safe. Particularly if he was right about her identity.

She strode across the room to the suit of armor, bent its left arm up and lifted the face mask. Then she bent the right knee forward. The breastplate opened outward with a slight scrape of metal revealing a safe in the figure's middle.

"Cute. I wonder how long it would take an experienced thief to find that?"

She sniffed. "You barely noticed him. What does that say about your expertise? Don't just stand there, open it."

Spencer crossed to stand beside her. "I don't think so."

She spun around, so close the flashlight hit him on the arm. Her lips parted slightly as he lifted it from her fingers. They were very nice lips, he noticed. Soft and full. Perfect for kissing.

"What do you mean, you don't think so?" she demanded. "Do you know how to open it or not?" Her eyes widened as she gazed at him. He took a step forward and she tried to take a step back. The knight refused to yield.

Spencer closed the inches that separated them by placing his gloved hand against the knight's chest beside her head, effectively pinning her between them. "What do you want from inside?" he asked softly.

"What difference does it make? You're a burglar. So burgle already."

Her voice sounded breathless. He had a strong urge to taste that breath. To sample the texture of those lips. Instead, he adjusted his glasses beneath the ski mask with the thumb of his other hand. Another part of his body could use some adjusting as well, he thought wryly.

"Look, all I want is a piece of paper," she told him quickly. "You can have everything else we find inside."

That diverted his attention. "What's on the paper, Kerry?"

Her gaze skated about the room uneasily. "That's none of your business. What kind of a burglar are you?"

"A careful one."

"Great. Just great. A careful burglar. I don't have time for this. Are you going to open that safe or not?"

Actually, opening the safe wasn't a half-bad idea. The painting he needed to find could easily be rolled up small enough to fit inside. The only problem was, he had no clue how to crack a safe.

"Never mind," she said in exasperation. "Just move aside and let me try. Hadden could be back any minute."

"Why don't you simply ask him for the paper?"

She had the most expressive eyes, he thought, as guilt made her look away briefly. Whatever this paper was, she didn't want her fiancé to know about it. Interesting. Then she raised a hand to push against his chest. The contact sent a wave of new awareness rushing through him.

"You're crowding me," she told him.

Her words sounded breathless. He knew the feeling. "I don't think I'd better tell you what you're doing to me," he responded.

The flash in her eyes warned him and he stepped back.

"Smart man."

She twisted away and pulled a stethoscope from a pocket somewhere in her sweatshirt.

"You're kidding, right?" he asked as he realized what she planned to do.

Her nose wrinkled in disgust. "You aren't the only one who watches television."

Spencer nearly argued when he realized how ludicrous this was. She had to be Hadden's fiancée, and if she wanted to break into his safe, far be it from Spencer to stop her. He had a job to do and this might be his only chance. He walked to the nearest wall and began to examine the paintings.

"What are you doing?" she asked.

"I like art, all right?"

"Pornography." Her voice carried contempt.

"Art," he corrected. "There's nothing pornographic in two people making love."

"Two people making love, no. Posing with multiple partners while having prurient sex…"

Studying the painting before him, Spencer decided she was right. Calling this one "art" was stretching things. "This one's prurient, all right," he agreed. "I'm not sure this is even anatomically possible."

"Will you be quiet? I'm trying to hear the tumblers."

Spencer could almost hear her blush. She held a tiny key-chain flashlight in her left hand while she rested the stethoscope against the lock.

"Do you have any idea what you're doing?"

"No. Now be quiet," she shushed him.

With a shrug, he went back to the paintings, smiling to himself. He wondered if Hadden had any idea what sort of woman he was engaged to. She was going to lead him on a merry dance unless he set down some rules right from the start. Of course, he'd probably need a whip and a chair to enforce them, Spencer thought wryly.

He moved around the room, aware of her the entire time. Several smaller prints were clustered about at random, but none was the nude he was looking for. He skipped the larger paintings until the scene over the bed caught his eye. Surely his grandmother hadn't seen *that*.

Spencer turned his attention to the dresser.

"What are you doing?" she demanded.

"Going through his drawers."

"Funny, you didn't strike me as the type."

It took him a minute to grasp her mocking innuendo.

"Did anyone ever tell you you have a sassy mouth?"

She turned from the safe in disgust. "This is never going to work."

"I could have told you that."

"Yeah, well, then, you open it."

"No."

She glared at him. "Fine. He must have the combination written down somewhere."

"Not necessarily." But she wasn't listening.

She headed for the sitting room and the heavy walnut desk he'd seen in there earlier. Since the painting he needed wasn't in obvious sight, Spencer trailed after her.

The large rolltop sat before a wide bookcase. Spencer didn't have to read the titles to know the sort of books that probably filled those shelves.

"It's locked," she said in frustration.

Spencer shrugged. "I suppose you want me to open that too?"

"Can you?"

Probably not, but her skepticism challenged him. He strode over and yanked on the handle as hard as he could. The flimsy little lock gave way with the sound of splintering wood. The noise startled both of them into immobility.

"Give me brains over brawn any time," she muttered. And they both heard someone running down the hall.

Spencer didn't hesitate. He gripped her arm and hauled her out onto the balcony.

"What are you doing?" she whispered.

"Getting us the hell out of here. Come on."

"I am not climbing down a tree."

"Fine. You're his fiancée. You explain what you were doing in here. Just leave me out of the discussion."

Spencer mounted the wrought-iron railing and reached for the tree limb, swinging himself up easily. She lifted her arms without another word and he pulled her up as well. She was a solidly built woman, he discovered, not some anorexic model.

A light went on in the master bedroom. Spencer scrambled down the tree thinking if he'd had this much adrenaline as a kid, the baby-sitter never would have needed to call the fire department.

He dropped to the ground as the light went on in the sitting room. Kerry nearly landed on top of him. He caught her body at the last second and hauled her against his chest beneath the balcony out of sight. Someone found the open door and stepped outside above them. Her heart pounded against his chest. Or maybe that was his heart. Neither of them breathed until the footsteps retreated.

"Run!" Spencer whispered.

She spun from his arms and sprinted toward the back of the house with a graceful loping stride. He curbed an insane impulse to go with her. As Hadden's fiancée, she had every right to be running around the grounds. The only rights he had were the ones the police would read him if he was caught.

Spencer turned and raced in the opposite direction toward the fence where he'd entered.

His grandmother was going to be most unhappy.

2

THE MAN WAS CAUSING her no end of grief. Brenna Wolford stared at the picture of Hadden Summerton III and dropped the society section of the newspaper in annoyance.

She'd known Hadden since childhood. His grandfather had brokered her grandfather's paintings forever. But she disliked the social scene where Hadden and his crowd thrived. Oh, she could move about in it easily enough, and did so, since courting clients was occasionally part of her job as a planning analyst, but she found little in common with most of the people she met this way.

"Brenna?"

"In here, Grandpa. In the kitchen."

He carried the scent of turpentine and paint into the room with him. No need to ask how he'd spent the early morning hours.

"How's your work going?" she asked fondly.

His eyes narrowed as he spotted the newspaper picture. "My work is fine," he told her firmly, "but if I'd known you invited yourself down here for the weekend to go after that damned painting, I would have told you not to come."

His gruff words didn't intimidate her. "You don't mean that."

"Do so." But his expression softened as he reached for a coffee mug. "You said you wanted to come for a visit so you could attend Kerry and Hadden's engagement party. I can't believe you took such a risk, sneaking inside the estate last night. I'm sorry I ever told you about that painting."

Brenna tapped the newspaper. "I did come for the party. Kerry's been my friend since college, you know that."

Her grandfather snorted, unmollified. He knew she'd introduced Kerry and Hadden and was thrilled when the two of them hit if off.

"I was certain when I asked Hadden to sell me the painting he would," she continued. "When he told me he couldn't sell anything until after the entire collection was appraised…well, what was I supposed to do?" she asked. "I couldn't tell him why I really needed the painting. Your career is at stake, Grandpa. Your entire reputation."

He stopped in the act of reaching for the coffee-maker. "Brenna, at seventy-seven, I think my reputation can stand a few scars."

"You know better," she argued, standing eye to eye with him. "When word gets out that you once forged another man's name to one of your paintings and sold it—"

"Now, Brenna, they may not discover the forgery." He chewed on his lower lip, a sure sign he was more worried than he pretended.

"Who do you think you're kidding?" she asked gently. "As soon as the appraisers see that nude they're going to know you painted it—not some second-rate artist like Lispkit. You're internationally famous." She bumped her hip against the kitchen table and frowned at the newspaper.

"Don't forget," she continued, warming to her subject, "Hadden owns several of your paintings. I even saw a couple of your smaller landscapes on his dining room wall. The appraisers will have plenty of your work to compare with the nude. Plus, you painted it over one of your other works."

"Now, Brenna—"

"Don't now-Brenna me. The irony is, the nude would be worth three times more if you'd signed your own name instead of Lispkit's."

Benjamin Wolford rubbed the side of his nose leaving a streak of cerulean blue down the side. "That, my dear, is called poetic justice. Back when I painted that nude, my paintings weren't worth a cup of coffee—and I did so like my coffee."

He sighed and shook his shaggy head from side to side as he resumed his interrupted reach for the steaming coffee. "Lispkit was quite popular when I was young. The forged painting sold for enough money to give all three of us a much needed start."

His eyes took on a faraway stare. "Regina made a fabulous subject. I only signed Lispkit's name because Hadden had a buyer willing to pay a fortune for a Lispkit nude. Even split three ways, that money was enough to keep me in art supplies until my early work started selling."

"You would have been famous no matter what," she told him loyally. "How come you never married her?"

"Regina?" Her grandfather's expression turned bittersweet and he shifted his weight from foot to foot. "We wanted different things, I'm afraid. She wanted marriage and children right away, but I was obsessed with becoming a famous artist."

He stared at the dark brew in his mug as if it held some mystic meaning. "Regina and I drifted apart after Hadden sold the painting. She was furious with us, even though the money was a godsend for her too."

"Did you ever see her again?"

His shaggy head swung slowly. "No. I'm afraid she married a young minister a few years later."

Brenna watched her grandfather walk to the refrigerator, pour a bit of cream into his mug and then reach for the chocolate cheesecake. He loved New-York-style cheesecake, so she always brought one with her whenever she came for a visit. He quirked an eyebrow in her direction to ask if she wanted a piece and she shook her head quickly.

She couldn't help speculating about the nature of the relationship between her grandfather and Regina Linnington. She'd seen a picture of the woman once in a weathered snapshot her grandfather kept in a box of old photographs.

"The point is, Grandpa, we have to get that painting before the deception is discovered."

Again, her grandfather shook his head. "There's nothing more we can do. I stopped worrying about that painting coming to light years ago." He cut a huge slice of the cake. "Sure you don't want some?"

Brenna shook her head.

"Hadden tried to buy it back for years, but it had changed hands several times," he continued. "I was frankly surprised and relieved the day he called to tell me he'd finally acquired the thing. If he hadn't suffered that unfortunate heart attack, I'm certain he would have sold it back to me. We were supposed to meet for lunch the day they buried him, you know."

Brenna laid a hand on his arm. "You miss him."

"We were friends."

The simple words conveyed his grief. Brenna sought to change the subject. "Well, your friend had interesting taste in art, Grandpa. After seeing the stuff in his bedroom..."

"His erotica, you mean?"

"You know about that?"

Her grandfather's hearty chuckle dispelled the sadness. "Hadden was a randy bastard, but there was no harm in the man. Regina used to put him in his place all the time. She always said he was more show than go, though he did cut quite a swath through the ladies in his lifetime."

"Uh-huh." She frowned skeptically. "Well, that particular art collection certainly makes finding a specific nude more difficult." She tapped her fingernails against the tabletop. "And we're running out of time, Grandpa."

"Brenna, you're a joy and a dear and I love you more than anything, but enough is enough. We'll just have to wait and see what happens."

No way. Brenna was far from ready to give up. She watched him fork up a large bite of cheesecake. "Frank could have helped me get that painting out of the estate."

Benjamin Wolford set his fork down with a clatter, bumping his coffee mug and sending liquid sloshing onto the countertop. "Don't you even think about calling your brother."

Brenna decided not to tell him she'd already tried. Her much older half-brother was a Navy SEAL currently stationed in San Diego not far from their father and his third wife.

Frank hadn't been available when she'd called. Brenna had briefly debated telling their father about the painting, but he was busy raising his new family. The twin boys were only seven and her half-sister was three. Besides, the problem was here in Maryland. What could either of them do from California?

For that matter, what more could *she* do?

"Your career and your reputation will be in shreds when they identify that painting," she stewed.

Her grandfather set his plate down and leaned back

against the counter to sip from his mug. "Sooner or later, everyone pays for their mistakes, Brenna. You know that."

She knew, she just didn't like it. Her grandfather was the only real stability in her life. He'd been there through her parents' divorce when she was thirteen. He'd been there when her father moved across country with his new bride. And he'd been there for every one of the six times her lovable, flighty mother had selected a new husband.

Her grandfather's happy but pragmatic outlook never failed to lift Brenna's spirits and help her find balance in her own life.

"You took a tremendous risk last night," he admonished. "What if you'd been caught?"

She thought about the inept burglar and smiled. She hadn't told her grandfather about the other intruder. He'd have conniptions if he knew that somewhere, a professional thief knew exactly what she looked like— even if the thief had mistaken her for the younger Hadden's fiancée.

Visions of the tall dark stranger had slid in and out of her dreams all night. She kept wondering what he looked like beneath the ski mask, almost glad she didn't know. He had a great voice, rich and deeply sensual. Not to mention a terrific body. Dressed in sexy dark clothing, his jeans fitting the way men's jeans ought to fit, any woman would be happy to let him invade her dreams.

Brenna remembered the ease with which he'd lifted her into the tree and caught her when she jumped. She was no lightweight, despite watching her diet, but he'd moved her around like some petite china doll.

He might be an inept burglar, but he was strong.

And sexy.

Too sexy.

How could she ever forget the feel of his hardening body pressed against hers? She shook off the disturbing memory, consoling herself with the thought that no doubt his face would have been a disappointment.

"So, do we have a deal?" her grandfather asked, jarring her attention back to his seamed features. "You'll leave well enough alone?"

She smiled reassuringly. "What else can I do? I looked at all the paintings on his bedroom walls and the public areas downstairs. It must be somewhere else in the house. Want to teach me how to crack a safe? It could be rolled up and stored inside something, you know."

He touched the tip of her nose. "Not a chance even if I knew how."

"Didn't think so. And you've got paint on the side of your nose and probably on your finger as well."

He looked down and frowned. "Sorry. I didn't get any on you, did I?"

She wiped at her nose and her knuckle came away clean.

"Nope, and I have to run. I need a new pair of shoes for tonight."

"Got a date?"

"No."

He frowned. "You aren't still pining after that boring Todd creature, are you?"

Brenna laughed at the reminder of her stodgy almost-fiancé and only lover. In retrospect, she couldn't believe she'd dated Todd, let alone thought about marrying him. Fortunately, Brenna had been offered a huge promotion that meant moving to New York City. Todd couldn't believe she'd choose a job over marriage, but the decision had been easy.

"He was a bore, wasn't he?" She certainly couldn't

picture Todd climbing in through someone's window in the dead of night.

Her grandfather's face split in a grin. "You need someone who knows how to take a risk now and again. Someone who can enjoy life."

Again, Brenna thought of her burglar.

"Aren't there any men in New York? You deserve to have fun," he continued, "do something a little wild and reckless."

"Like break into Hadden's estate?" she teased.

"Your parents should have spanked you when you were small," he growled, but his eyes glowed with humor.

"When I find an original like you, Grandpa, I'll let you know."

Brenna considered the men she'd dated recently. Nice men she'd met through friends at work. Not one of them was an original. None created any sparks. The burglar had set off more sensual alarms than anyone else in her entire life. And she didn't even know what he looked like!

"You won't find a man sitting at home, you know," her grandfather continued, finishing off the slice of cheesecake with obvious relish.

She thought about the man she'd found the night before in Hadden Summerton's bedroom, and grinned. She wondered what her grandfather would think if she brought him home.

"You're probably right, Grandpa, but this is the nineties. Haven't you heard? Women don't need men anymore."

Her grandfather's retort was short and to the point. She kissed his paint-free cheek. "See you later."

"I DIDN'T GET IT," Spencer Griffen told his grandmother without preamble.

"That's all right, dear."

He gripped the telephone receiver more tightly and stared out the sliding glass door leading to his balcony. "No, it isn't, and we both know it. When that painting is revealed, the press will have a field day."

"Spencer, everyone has done something in their life they wish they could undo, but a painting of me in the nude is far from the end of the world. The pose isn't obscene, you know."

"Of course not! But you're about to be named the chief spokesperson for the child pornography committee, not to mention being the widow of a world-famous minister."

"Now, dear, you've done everything you can..."

Spencer's gaze drifted to the open box his sister had left on his dining-room table. He wondered what his grandmother would say if she could see the contents.

Spencer lifted the pair of padded handcuffs on top and fingered them absently. Knowing his grandmother's sense of humor, she'd probably make some outrageous comment and then scold them. But if a member of the child pornography committee saw the contents of this box, they'd be hunting for a new spokesperson immediately, convinced his grandmother's entire family was morally bankrupt.

"I haven't tried everything," he interrupted, setting the handcuffs back inside, on top of a wildly improbable vibrator. "There's Hadden's engagement party tonight."

"Spencer, I do not want you taking any more chances."

He could practically see her finger waggling. And for some reason he pictured the woman he'd found under the bed. Taking chances with her might be worth a risk or two. Except that she was already engaged, he reminded himself, and that put her strictly off limits.

"You won't help my campaign by getting arrested, Spencer."

"I have no intention of getting arrested," he assured her. "Don't worry, I met someone who can get me inside the estate without questions being asked." *If* he was very lucky and worked things right. "I'll just mingle with the rest of the guests until I find your painting. Piece of cake."

"People have been known to choke on a piece of cake, Spencer," she told him sternly. "Particularly when they try to steal it."

He found himself grinning at her analogy. "Don't worry, I'll be fine."

"It's a grandmother's prerogative to worry."

"And you're very good at it," he assured her, "but we only have a couple of days left. I have to find that Lispkit original before the press connects your very well-known face to that of the woman in the painting."

His grandmother's silence told him that, despite her protests, she was concerned about the impact the painting might have on her pet project—more concerned than she wanted to let on. Spencer knew it wasn't her own reputation that worried her. She just didn't want any negativity associated with a campaign that she believed in with every fiber of her being.

His grandmother had lived in her famous husband's shadow for many years, offering unstinting support and quietly doing whatever needed doing, particularly in the area of children's needs. Now that the limelight was focused on her, Spencer wasn't about to let years of effort be destroyed because she'd once posed for a starving artist.

"No one may ever connect me with that painting, Spencer."

"No one ever *will* connect you," he promised. "I'm going to do whatever it takes to make sure of that. I'll call you as soon as I have the painting."

As he replaced the receiver, Spencer wondered if his tuxedo would need pressing. He was pretty sure he'd picked it up from the cleaner's after Sylvia dumped the champagne on him...or had that been Alison? Well, whoever he'd taken to the play's opening at the Kennedy Center.

He'd have to call Liz and reschedule tonight's date. She would not be happy. He'd need to send flowers. And wasn't Alison's picnic tomorrow? He reached for the calendar hanging beside the phone. Good thing he had an account with the florist. He'd better clear his social obligations for the entire weekend just to be safe.

If only that mouthy little thing under the bed hadn't nearly got them caught last night. He grinned at the memory, then his gaze flicked to the note on the table that his sister had left along with the box.

Hey, Valentino, hope you don't mind but I can't leave this sort of stuff lying around the house for my kids to find. I'll be by to get it sometime Saturday.

The note was signed with a lipstick smear at the bottom.

Big sisters could be a real pain.

Valentino, indeed. Spencer was annoyed by the nickname. He didn't have *that* many women friends, but his family did like to tease him about having a harem. Of course, he'd never been thrilled with his real name either. On the bright side, his mother, the movie buff, hadn't been a big fan of silent movies or he could have been stuck with a name like Rudolph.

Now if he could just turn a little of his so-called

charm on Kerry, maybe he could keep her rattled enough to get him inside the estate tonight. He really didn't want to be climbing any more trees—particularly in a tuxedo.

THE GROUNDS of the Summerton estate were lit as if for a Hollywood premiere when Brenna drove up. Hadden had pulled out all the stops. Brenna handed a young valet her key and stepped from the car, smoothing the calf-length skirt of her dress. A figure suddenly detached itself from the bushes and joined her as she started up the steps.

She whirled in alarm when he took her arm. Before she could react, his voice and the subtle scent of his aftershave identified him.

"I thought you were never going to get here," he murmured.

"You!"

"Good. You remember me. As the fiancée, I thought you would be one of the first to arrive."

Her imagination hadn't done the thief justice. If she'd seen the face that went with his voice and body she never would have slept at all last night. He wore glasses, but they did nothing to detract from his ruggedly handsome looks. Superman playing Clark Kent.

Dreaming about his body in black jeans and a leather jacket had been bad enough, but now that she'd seen him in a tuxedo...

"What are you doing here?" she managed to ask.

"Waiting for you, of course."

"Are you out of your mind?"

His smile was wide and disarming. "I think you raised that possibility last night."

"You can't go inside with me!"

"Well, I can hardly get in without you. No invitation."

"I don't believe this."

"Actually, I'm not sure I do either, but what the heck." His shoulders rose and fell briefly. They were nice wide shoulders. "Who better to get me inside a party than the guest of honor?"

Oh, Lord, he still thought she was Kerry. She stumbled on the top step and he caught her, his hand branding her arm through the silk of her dress. He smiled and she felt that smile clear to her toenails. No man should have such a sensual smile.

The guard at the door reached for her invitation, glanced at it, and ushered them inside before she could protest. Oh, well, what difference would it make? She had no doubt that if he hadn't walked in the front door with her now, the thief would have climbed through a window later.

"The bride-to-be needs an invitation to her own party?" the burglar questioned with raised eyebrows.

"Everyone needs an invitation," she managed to mutter. "It keeps out the riffraff." What would he do when he realized she wasn't Kerry?

"Like me?"

When had his arm snaked its way around her waist? He pulled her entirely too close to his lean, hard body. Close enough to inhale more of his aftershave. Close enough to resurrect some primitive responses she didn't expect or want.

"What are you doing here?" she asked, desperately trying to draw back without being obvious. He was doing this to rile her.

"Finishing what you so rudely interrupted last night."

"What *I* interrupted?"

His eyes twinkled behind the lenses of his glasses. He'd make hash of her common sense if she let him.

"I didn't interrupt a thing," she insisted. "You can't

mean to go back upstairs. Not tonight. Not with the house full of people."

Not when that was exactly what she had planned to do herself.

"Of course I can. It's the perfect time. Don't worry, as you said, Hadden's insured. And speaking of the devil, here he comes now. Excuse me while I pretend to get you something to drink."

He melted into a large group standing beside them. Hadden reached her before she had time to convince herself she didn't miss the arm around her waist or the burglar's solid presence at her side.

Normally, Hadden was exactly her height, five foot ten, but when he hugged her, Brenna realized tonight he wore lifts that added a couple of inches. She hid her smile as he stepped back to smooth the pencil-thin mustache he'd recently grown. The thin wispy pale hairs added nothing to his slightly puffy round face, nor did they disguise the fact that his white-blond hair was thinning in front.

Why was it men who couldn't grow hair on top of their heads so often tried to make up for the lack by growing it on their faces?

"I'm glad you're here, Brenna," Hadden greeted. "Kerry had a sudden problem with her dress. She asked me to find her sister. Unfortunately, her sister doesn't appear to be here yet. Do you think you could help? I can't leave with all these guests arriving."

"Ah, sure. Of course."

"Thanks. Top of the stairs, first door on the left."

She headed for the wide staircase, not sure whether to bless her luck or curse it. This wasn't quite the way she had envisioned getting back upstairs tonight. And where had the sexy burglar disappeared to?

Brenna turned the upstairs corner to find her red-haired friend in a doorway, wringing her hands. Her glittery blue dress slumped from one shoulder. "Oh, Brenna, I'm so glad you're here! I've got a terrible problem. My zipper broke. Will you take a look and see if we can fix it?"

Brenna followed her inside, realizing Kerry was nearly in tears. The long blue zipper on the sequined gown had broken all right. Even a dozen safety pins wouldn't be enough to salvage the lovely dress.

"Not without a sewing machine and a new zipper."

"What am I going to do?" Kerry wailed. She pushed back the tangle of fiery curls that framed her face. Kerry hated her kinky orange hair, as she called it, almost as much as the freckles that she spent hours trying to cover with makeup.

"Do you have another dress?" Brenna asked.

"Not with me. I came early in my jeans to supervise the caterers."

Brenna studied her friend's build. "Well, we'll just have to switch outfits. I know my dress isn't as flashy as that sequined number you're wearing, but I think we can make it work temporarily."

"I can't take your dress!"

"Why not? I'm not the bride-to-be. No one came here to see me. You can wear this downstairs while someone goes to your place for another dress. I'll just wait here in your jeans and blouse."

"Brenna, I can't ask you—"

"You aren't asking. I'm offering."

"But you're taller."

"And this hits me mid-calf, which means it should reach your ankles. It'll be a little loose on top, and we may have to tape the sleeves, but it will only be for a short time." She tugged at her zipper, quickly stripping off the black dress.

"Oh, Brenna, I can't believe you're doing this. How can I thank you?"

Feeling guilty because of her ulterior motive, Brenna forced a smile. "I don't need thanks. To tell you the truth, big parties aren't really my idea of fun."

"I know. Yet you came all the way from New York to be here tonight anyhow. You're a good friend," Kerry said, giving her a hug. "So, what about your date?"

"Date?"

"You did bring one, didn't you?"

Had Kerry seen her come in with the burglar?

"Oh, uh, don't worry. John will be fine on his own for a while. He knows I came up here to help you. He won't miss me."

"But what about you? I can't just leave you here alone."

"Well, I could always go and look at the infamous art collection Hadden's grandfather is supposed to have kept in his bedroom," she said, trying for an unconcerned tone.

Kerry giggled. "Oh, yes. You really have to see that stuff. It's wild."

"Would it be okay with Hadden, do you think?"

"Are you kidding? He won't mind at all after the favor you're doing for me. Brenna, you're a lifesaver."

Guilt threatened to choke her. "Not at all. Here, let me help you get into that dress."

Once Kerry left, Brenna slumped back against the nearest wall. Fate could be amazing.

After pulling on Kerry's snug denims and her long-sleeved blouse, Brenna discovered the blouse gaped on her and she had to leave the snap undone on the jeans in order to breathe. She grimaced at her reflection in the mirror. Her fancy French twist and the sparkly crystal earrings made the too-small shirt and jeans look all the more ludicrous on her. Good thing no one else would see her dressed like this.

Her new high heels were not only absurd, but they pinched her toes, so Brenna hurried along the hall to the master bedroom in her stocking feet. Unfortunately, someone had locked the door—and also the one leading into the sitting room. She glared at the wood panel in annoyance. Hadden probably didn't want his guests wandering up here staring at the erotica. Or maybe he'd locked the door because of the break-in last night. Either way, fate was being tricky with its gifts.

Frustrated, she tried the bedroom next to Hadden's. That door wasn't locked, so she took a few minutes to study the walls. Not a nude anywhere. She headed for the balcony.

The balconies were separated by a wrought-iron divider with climbing ivy that grew from planters on both sides, and the large maple tree by the house, which "John" had used the night before to swing himself, then her, off the balcony, did bend conveniently close. She studied the situation and decided if she could climb down the tree, she could climb around this small barrier. In fact, the tree limb would give her something to balance against. With luck, Hadden wouldn't have fixed the broken window and she could enter the sitting room through the sliding glass door.

Luck, it seemed, had moved on. Brenna swayed, clutching the wrought-iron divider as her foot searched valiantly for purchase on the other side. Kerry's jeans wouldn't let her stretch far enough no matter how she struggled. Brenna became uncomfortably conscious of the sounds emanating from the party below as her right foot began to cramp on the railing.

"I don't believe this," she muttered in frustration.

"Me either."

She swayed in shock as her burglar moved out of the deep shadows at the far end of Hadden's balcony and strode forward. Strong arms circled her waist. Seemingly without effort, he pulled her to safety and allowed her body to slide along the length of his.

She stared at his glasses, finding she couldn't remember what color his eyes were. For some reason, that seemed important. Maybe because his lips were so close to her own. Dangerously close. "You scared me," she told him on a shaky breath.

"Lady, that's nothing compared to what you just did to me. Do you realize you could have fallen and broken your pretty little neck?"

She couldn't pull her gaze from him, despite knowing that she should.

"What are you doing here?" he demanded. "You're supposed to be downstairs."

"So are you." She tried to step back, but his arms didn't release her. She was extremely conscious of every hard muscle pressed against her.

"And where did you get that outfit?" he snarled.

"Why? Were you thinking of buying one?"

She caught the flash of his smile.

"You really do have the sassiest damn mouth."

And he released her, stepping back.

"So what are you doing here?" he asked.

"Don't worry. I have permission."

"Permission." He tipped his head to one side as if studying a rare specimen. "To climb onto the balcony?"

"Well, not exactly, but it is okay for me to look around."

"Sure. That's why you're out here in a pair of tight jeans and an open blouse with a hundred or more of your closest friends downstairs in fancy dress to help celebrate your engagement."

About to protest, Brenna followed the path his gaze had taken and found most of the buttons had come undone on Kerry's blouse. She was glad he couldn't see her blush in the darkness as she hastily rebuttoned the blouse. "I wasn't expecting to be seen by anyone."

Noise from the party carried to where they stood. That was when she noticed the broken window had been repaired.

"Oh, no. They fixed it. Can you get us inside again?" she asked, gesturing toward the door.

"What happened to your 'permission.'"

"Permission, I have. A key, I don't have."

He pushed against the bridge of the glasses spanning his nose. "Right. How foolish of me."

"Are we going to stand out here all night, or are you going to do your burglar thing and get us inside?"

"Oh, inside, definitely. Since you have 'permission' and all."

"You know, you can be really aggravating at times."

"I'm taking lessons from you." He turned away and withdrew the glass cutter and the suction cup from inside his jacket before she could think of a snappy comeback. He wore gloves again, she realized. She should have thought to do the same. Too late now. Besides, Kerry had told her she could go inside and look around.

"That's pretty neat."

"Yeah. Let's just hope they didn't have time to rig this window with an alarm or your 'permission' is going to be put to the test. We'll see how much Hadden really loves you if we get caught."

"Don't worry about it," she said bravely. "I don't intend to get caught."

"Neither do I, lady." He reached his hand through the hole and opened the door. "After you."

She stepped quickly inside the dark sitting room and ran smack into a small table. Only his fast reflexes kept a lamp from toppling to the floor.

"Take it easy, will you?"

"Sorry, but I can't see a thing. Turn on the light."

"We can't do that."

"Of course we can. You just press that little switch. See? Light. I told you, it will be all right, even if we're caught in here."

Blinking in the sudden glow, he glared at her. "Maybe for you, but I don't fancy doing ten to life in a state penitentiary."

"Is that what the penalty is?"

He looked startled. "How the hell would I know?"

"I just figured, this being your line of work and all…"

She didn't hear what he muttered, but decided it was probably for the best. Pretending to ignore him, Brenna crossed the room and unlocked the hall door in case she needed to make a fast escape. Then she headed to the desk. "Oh, good. At least they didn't fix this lock. Maybe I can find the combination in here now."

He was back to staring at the pictures again so she began rummaging through the desk and its contents. "You could help, you know," she told him when she realized how many papers were inside the top three drawers, not to mention all the cubby holes.

"What I'm looking for won't be in the desk."

That got her attention. "What are you looking for?" she asked.

"Never mind."

"Fine. I need to get inside the safe even if you don't."

He stopped to study the painting on the wall next to

the desk. Brenna glanced at it and felt a blush steal up her cheeks as her brain accepted what she saw.

"Interesting variation," he said.

"Looks uncomfortable to me."

He chuckled, a low, pleasing sound that sent currents of electricity along her nerve endings.

"Oh, I don't know, might be fun," he suggested.

"If you like fruit."

"I love fruit." His gaze traveled slowly down to her chest. "And sexy black lingerie."

The blouse, she realized, gaped open again. He had a clear view of her fancy lace bra and the rounded tops of her breasts. Heat flamed her cheeks as she twisted to one side, doing up the buttons with unsteady fingers.

"A gentleman would have pretended not to notice."

"Only if he was dead or gay."

Laughter in his voice, he strode into the bedroom, turned on a light, and paused in front of the armor knight. "How do you get this thing open again?"

She followed on shaky legs, grateful for the change in topic. "What difference does it make? I thought you couldn't get inside the safe."

"I never said I couldn't."

No, he never had, exactly. He'd just refused to open it for her. When he continued to stand there, she told him how to move the arm and leg. Minutes later, she heard the distinctive click as the tumblers fell into place and the safe sprang open.

"How did you do that?"

"Oh, even we inept idiots have our uses."

"I never said...okay, maybe I did, but you have to admit, you weren't acting very professional last night."

"Oh? You hang out with professional thieves on a regular basis?"

She ignored his gibe. "You must have found the combination."

"You could say that."

"Where?" she demanded. "On that painting?"

"Let's just say that you and the painting gave me an idea and it worked."

She glared at him, knowing she would never look at a bowl of fruit the same way again.

"Safes usually have number combinations that go left, right, left," he told her. "Look around this room and tell me what three numbers come to mind."

Brenna glanced around and shook her head. Nothing at all came to her mind except that he looked sinfully sexy in that tuxedo, which was not the sort of thought she wanted to be having at this particular moment.

"Does 36-24-36 sound familiar?"

"Move aside," she commanded in exasperation. His chuckle sent a tingle clear through her as he stepped away from the safe.

"Be my guest."

The contents were less than thrilling. A wad of cash lay inside a leather pouch, and three boxes of what looked like expensive jewelry were stacked alongside an assortment of papers. No canvas, rolled or flat.

"Blast! I was so sure it would be in here."

"Don't like jewelry, huh?"

"I'm not here to steal anything," she admonished. "I just need something that belongs to me."

"Uh-huh. You said something about a paper? I notice there's a whole stack inside."

"Yes, but—"

A muffled voice carried clearly from the hall, calling out a name in a questioning tone. Their eyes met in mutual panic.

"Lock the safe! I'll stall her." Brenna darted past

him and ran through the connecting room to open the door from the sitting room to the hall.

"Kerry?" she called softly.

Her friend turned around in relief. "Oh, there you are. I don't think my blouse is a great fit on you. The buttons are undone."

Brenna fumbled with the recalcitrant buttons, aware of her burning cheeks and hoping Kerry would think the buttons were the reason why. "You did say it was okay if I looked at the art?" she asked.

"Oh, sure. No problem. Hadden won't care. He's got the appraisers coming out on Monday. They're going to catalogue everything. Then he's going to put most of that stuff on the auction block."

Her gaze moved past Brenna to something over her shoulder. Her blue eyes widened in feminine appreciation.

"Oh, hello, there. I didn't realize she wasn't alone. You must be John."

3

DUMBSTRUCK, BRENNA turned and found the intruder leaning enticingly against the doorjamb.

"I guess I must be," the thief agreed easily.

"Uh, nice to meet you, John."

Kerry's face turned bright pink, and Brenna knew why. Between the man at her back, the erotic art, and Brenna's partially unbuttoned blouse and slacks, there was no doubt what Kerry thought they'd been doing. And there was nothing Brenna could do or say to correct the impression.

"Sorry to interrupt," Kerry told him, then turned to Brenna. "Looks like I shouldn't have worried about leaving you on your own. I just wanted you to know my sister ran over to my place. It'll probably take her ten minutes or so. Okay?"

"Of course."

"I'll make sure no one else disturbs you."

Brenna wanted to cover her face with her hands.

"Nice meeting you, John," Kerry said again with a wave and quickly started back down the hall.

"You too," the thief replied. He sounded amused.

Brenna gave him a shove back inside and shut the door. "Why did you let her see you?"

"How was I to know she wasn't going to come bursting in here? I figured it would look better if it seemed like you were just showing me around."

"Better to who?"

"Look, if you're worried about Hadden—"

"I am *not* worried about Hadden."

He looked quizzical. "You're not?"

"No."

"You do know your friend thinks we were—"

"I know exactly what she thinks!" Brenna took a deep breath and closed her eyes. "She won't say anything to Hadden."

"Uh-huh. Well, this probably isn't a good time to mention this, but your blouse is open again. You might as well take it off."

She looked down and groaned. "Someone wake me."

"Afraid that won't happen, unless we're sharing…"

Brenna straightened up.

"…the same nightmare," he added with a devilish smile that halted the flow of air to her lungs.

"I am not sharing anything with you," she told him, jamming an index finger against his solid chest for emphasis.

His smile widened. "Too bad. There are a couple of really interesting variations in some of these paintings that I wouldn't mind exploring. Take that scene by the waterfall—"

"Never mind!" She couldn't look any higher than his chest. It was such a nice chest. "Why don't you go downstairs and steal the silverware?"

"Too heavy. Besides, the market for silver isn't what it used to be."

"Then what are you doing here?"

He crossed the room, lifted a picture of two women from the wall, and turned it over.

"Looking at erotic art, at the moment."

"Do help yourself." She thought she heard him chuckle as he replaced one painting and turned over another one. "What are you looking *for?*" she demanded.

"I just wanted to be sure there wasn't something more interesting hidden behind any of these."

"You mean like another painting?" She hadn't thought of that possibility.

His head jerked in her direction. "Why did you say that?"

"What?"

His expression held none of its usual amusement. "About another painting."

Oh, no. She'd given herself away. Brenna turned toward the waterfall painting and tried to sound nonchalant. "Well, what else could you be looking for behind the pictures? It can't be the safe combination since you already got that open."

He tipped his head to study her. "I did, didn't I?"

She didn't breathe until he continued prowling the room. Trying not to be obvious, she watched him turn over picture after picture. What would she do if he discovered the one she needed?

"Tell me something," he said, finally. "Do you and Hadden have one of those 'open' relationships?"

Oh, boy, murky water. How long before he realized she wasn't Kerry? "No."

"You just like to play around behind his back?"

"No!"

He paused, an exceptionally graphic painting in his hands. One of the men in the painting bore a faint resemblance to her thief with his dark good looks, broad chest, and an equally broad... She swallowed, tearing her gaze from the image.

"Your friend certainly didn't seem shocked to find us in such a compromising situation. Embarrassed, maybe," he continued, thankfully unaware of her distraction. "What's going on here, Kerry? What are you doing up here dressed like this? Not that I'm complaining about that blouse, mind you."

Brenna looked down quickly, found all the buttons were where they belonged, and summoned a glare. He replaced the picture of the obscenely but happily subservient woman and her three towering males, and walked over to stand before the large group picture hanging over the bed.

"Could you give me a hand here?" he asked as he reached up to tug at the frame.

She brushed past the metal knight and grabbed the opposite corner of the frame as he attempted to lift the large painting.

"This isn't moving," she said. "I think it must be bolted to the wall."

"Yeah. Odd, don't you think?"

Odd didn't begin to describe anything that had happened since she snuck inside the estate the night before.

"What's odd about bolting a frame to the wall that must weigh sixty pounds? If it fell, it would kill someone."

"Hmm, death by orgy. Interesting epitaph."

"Do you have a name?" she asked, coming around the bed.

"Yep." He continued running his hands along the frame, abruptly standing on the bed, trampling the pillows and the black satin comforter.

"Don't be cute. And get down from there. You're making a mess. What am I supposed to call you?"

He tipped his head to the side and one of his deadly grins appeared. "You seemed to like John, and that works for me. How about you?"

"Fine," she said, completely exasperated with the entire situation. "Look, *John*, I don't think we have much more time in here and that picture isn't going to budge. What do you say you get back downstairs—"

They heard the sitting-room door open.

He dropped to the mattress, reaching for her at the same time. She tumbled forward to sprawl on top of him, unprepared when his lips immediately sought her mouth. It was an open, hungry, urgent assault.

The unexpected contact stole her breath. The heat of his kiss seared her brain, paralyzing all rational thought. He probed her mouth with his tongue, plunging inside when her lips yielded to his urgent demand. This was a kiss unlike any other. Her lips clung to his, but it was her own startling response that made the experience so unique. He inflamed needs and wants and passions she hadn't even realized had been lying dormant all this time. Her mind raced under the unexpected passionate assault.

Vaguely, she felt the hand that began to shape and caress her buttock. She arched into that caress, pushing herself against him, wanting more. His other hand held the back of her head in a way guaranteed to destroy her carefully constructed hairdo. She couldn't have cared less. His mouth was doing wicked things to hers, stirring to life all the buried passion within her.

She sensed his pleasure as he moved against her, the friction of his clothing not disguising the fact that he was all male, and fully aroused. His scent filled her nostrils, potent and wonderfully right.

In the back of her mind, Brenna knew she should be fighting, not succumbing to the crazy passions being fired by his mouth and his hands. Only, she couldn't seem to get enough of him. He tasted of spearmint gum, she discovered, as his tongue dared hers in a duel of bittersweet need.

She swept his shoulders with her hands, testing the strength of him with her fingers. His hand slid up her spine, a caress that pushed her more firmly against his hard length. The heady feeling was mind-boggling. No one had ever made her want like this.

Her panties dampened as her breasts swelled in anticipation of his caress.

"Oh. I'm sorry," a hesitant voice murmured from somewhere far away. "My sister's back. See you later." And the disembodied voice disappeared, closing the door.

Brenna froze. His lips blazed a path down her neck. She shuddered. Part of her never wanted him to stop. Part of her wanted to lie here on top of him, reveling in the pulsing feel of his body that left hers aching with desire. But another, saner portion of her brain protested. She didn't even know this man.

Brenna managed to plant her hands on his hard chest and raise herself away from him. "What are you doing?"

His smoky eyes gazed at her. "Kissing. Doesn't Hadden ever kiss you?"

He tried to pull her head back down, but she resisted. "Stop."

"Are you sure?" His hands loosened their hold, but his expression was still heavy with arousal.

"Yes." Brenna scrambled off him, and he let her go, watching with hooded eyes.

"You have wonderfully kissable lips," he said softly, seductively. "I thought so last night and I was right. By the way, your blouse is unbuttoned again."

Her fingers fumbled for the buttons, unable to insert them in the holes. She was stunned by her reaction to him. Another few seconds and they would have been making love.

"Allow me," he offered, sitting up and reaching out to do up the nearest button.

She stepped back. "Why did you do that?"

"So your friend would see what she expected to see."

Brenna trembled. "You're impossible."

"So I've been told."

"I need to get dressed."

"Better fix your hair, too," he told her, with what sounded suspiciously like masculine satisfaction.

"Be out of here before I return or I'm calling security," she huffed.

"Kerry?"

She hesitated, halfway to the sitting room, but she didn't dare turn around.

"You shouldn't marry him," he said, without any trace of amusement. "You've got too much passion for a wimp like Hadden."

She forced herself to the door, closing it with a gentle snick.

SPENCER WATCHED from the crowd as Kerry descended the staircase with her friend, back straight, head high, her grace obvious with each step she took. She again wore the simple black dress that made a man want to peel it slowly from her feminine body. She'd taken her hair down, he noted in satisfaction. It hung in long shimmering dark waves. The change made her regal bearing more ethereal. He couldn't seem to draw his eyes from her.

He wanted her, he admitted. The strength of that wanting shocked him. And the idea of her marrying Hadden Summerton III sat like a rock in his chest. He had nothing against Hadden. He didn't even know the man. But a woman finding satisfaction in another man's arms would never have responded to Spencer the way Kerry had upstairs.

Or was that just his ego kicking in?

Spencer frowned. He hadn't meant to get so carried

away up there. It must have been all that prurient art work and the glimpses of that sexy black bra.

He muttered a curse, knowing that he was lying to himself. Those hadn't been his only reasons for kissing her. He should leave right now. He'd already checked out all the paintings in the downstairs rooms. Lots of artists were represented, but no Lispkits were anywhere to be found. Whatever Hadden had done with his grandmother's painting, Spencer wasn't going to find it tonight. Hanging around the estate only increased his risk of being caught—and if he was caught, Kerry would be embroiled in his transgressions, thanks to the scene upstairs.

He regretted that fact, but not the events themselves. She was bold and sassy and sexy as hell. As he watched her come down that staircase he wondered what she'd do if he walked over, lifted her in his arms and carried her outside to finish what they'd started.

Hadden greeted her with an affectionate hug at the bottom of the stairs. They didn't act like lovers. In fact, the look Hadden gave the freckle-faced woman in the flashy green dress was distinctly predatory.

What was going on here? Had he made a mistake? Maybe she wasn't really Kerry after all. If she was, she deserved better than some wimpy Lothario with a wandering eye. Yet she seemed oblivious to what was going on between her companions as she studied the crowd.

Spencer wanted to think she was looking for him, but unless she planned to have him thrown out on his ear or arrested, he couldn't imagine that she'd want to see him again—unless she too wanted to finish what they'd begun upstairs.

Damn. This was ridiculous. If she was Kerry Martin, she was about to become officially engaged. That made her off-limits. Spencer wondered if she knew about the gossip running through the crowd.

According to rumor, Hadden's father, Hadden Junior, had done his best to run through the family fortune before dying in a race car accident several years ago. Hadden Senior had added to that burden by spending a lot of money on collecting art. If the rumors were true, Hadden III needed to sell the contents of the mansion to avoid a serious cash-flow problem.

And why the hell couldn't their respective mothers have found something original to name their sons? What sort of name was Hadden, anyhow?

Spencer fought down his irritation as the three across the room turned and headed for the solarium and the live band inside. Knowing better, he followed at a distance. When Hadden took Kerry, and not the redhead, into his arms, Spencer knew it was time to leave before he succumbed to a strange urge to plant a fist against that asinine mustache.

"John, there you are! I told her you hadn't left yet."

He whirled to find the short redhead approaching, an open smile on her round friendly face.

"I understand you have to leave early. A business engagement in the morning?"

Spencer shrugged, not certain how to respond. "You know how it is."

"Unfortunately, I do. Are you sure you can't stay a while longer? I understand Hadden plans to present the ring in a suitably dramatic fashion." Her freckled face grinned impishly up at him.

And his grandmother would say, it was just like Spencer not to notice that the woman he'd been kissing upstairs a few minutes ago hadn't been wearing a ring. He stared out at the crowded dance floor, trying without success to spot her.

The last thing he wanted to do was stick around to see Hadden place a ring on Kerry's finger.

"I have to go," he told the redhead, a bit more brusquely than he meant to. Her smile never wavered.

"Well, I hope your meeting is on a golf course and not inside a stuffy office. Tomorrow *is* a Saturday," she chided.

"So it is."

"I'm sorry I interrupted earlier."

She seemed genuinely sorry, which only added to his discomfort.

"No problem," he said uneasily.

Obviously, she saw nothing wrong with an engaged woman indulging herself with someone other than the groom-to-be. This social crowd had a different set of morals than he'd been raised with. He banked his annoyance, but knew that he was still frowning.

"That's quite a collection Hadden's grandfather has upstairs," he said in an effort to change the subject and be polite.

She giggled. "Isn't it just? I was shocked the first time I saw all that stuff. Did you go into the bathroom?"

"Uh…"

"Sartorial splendor at its best. Or is it its worst? Just once, before Hadden sells this place, I want to bathe in that tub."

"He's planning to sell the house?"

Her merry blue eyes twinkled up at him. "Thinking of buying?"

Was she flirting with him? Spencer wasn't quite sure. Her voice was playful, but her look teased without being sexual.

"I couldn't afford the taxes."

Bright orange hair drifted around her face and she pushed it back with a freckled hand, nodding seriously. "Neither can Hadden. This building is a monstrosity. The fuel bills alone are astronomical."

"Are they?"

"Heavens, yes, look at these high ceilings. You can't heat or cool a place this size efficiently. And all this art." Her hand swept the area to indicate the paintings and sculptures, he supposed. "I mean, some of it belongs in a museum, but the rest should go in the trash. I swear there's as much junk as not."

Spencer seized the opening she presented. "Is everything on display or is there an attic full?"

"Good grief, I hope not. The possibility is enough to make me shudder. There are already paintings and statues in every room. Hadden can't wait for the appraisers to get started next week."

"Surely everything is insured?"

Her flame-colored hair swished annoyingly from side to side. "Only partially. Grandpa Summerton didn't have the sort of security arrangement the insurance company felt he needed. If this place caught fire tomorrow, Hadden wouldn't get a quarter of the true value for most of the contents. In fact, there isn't even an accurate inventory."

"That seems rather foolish given the extent of his collection."

"You're telling me."

"So, what does Kerry think about selling everything?"

She looked startled for a second, then laughed. "*Kerry,*" she said, with unusual emphasis and a wide grin, "thinks its past time to get rid of the whole kit and caboodle. I mean, who wants to *live* in a museum? Fortunately, the devoted bridegroom will do anything to please her, you know."

Spencer glanced at the crowded dance floor and still couldn't spot the couple. But it occurred to him to wonder why, if Hadden would do anything to please Kerry, she'd been sneaking through the old man's safe? What did she need that she couldn't simply ask Hadden for?

"Anything, huh?" he said, feeling grim.

Her eyes sparkled. "Oh, yes. Everyone knows he's absolutely devoted to—"

"John!"

Out of the crowd on his left, in a swirl of black silk, Kerry appeared, sounding breathless. Anxiety pinched her features. "Are you leaving already?"

Hadden had been prevented from following her by an older couple who had impeded him physically, the lady taking his arm and chattering animatedly. Spencer decided he'd pushed his luck far enough. Time to go, before someone discovered the damaged patio door upstairs and started looking around for strangers.

He focused on Kerry's soft full lips, noting a hint of something that looked suspiciously like a whisker burn along her jawline. From him? Or had she and Hadden...?

"I need to go," he said abruptly. "It seems I have an early meeting tomorrow morning."

A faint blush stained her cheeks. Absently, she tucked a dark strand of hair back behind her ear. "Oh. Well, if you have to." She turned uncertainly to her friend who watched them, openly curious. "Uh, I think Hadden wanted to introduce you to those people."

The redhead blinked in surprise. Spencer's jaw clenched. Didn't Kerry know better than to throw her fiancé and her friend together? Hadn't she noticed the way Hadden ogled her?

Now the titian-haired vamp's expression went from puzzled to amused. She gave Kerry a knowing glance.

"You are definitely going to call me in the morning, right?"

Kerry blushed. "Right."

There was an undercurrent between the two women that left Spencer feeling like he'd opened a mystery novel in the middle. The dynamics between Kerry and Hadden and the redhead were all wrong. He just couldn't understand what was happening here.

"Bye, John." The redhead winked and turned away.

Her earlier conversation had just given him an idea. The half-baked plan was so outrageous and wild he should get himself committed for even considering it.

His gaze fastened on Kerry. He refused to be sidetracked by the alluring plumpness of her lips. He wondered what she'd say if she knew what he was thinking of doing.

All right, it was a crazy idea. He could get in serious trouble. But, somehow, he had to recover that painting before the appraisers showed up. Time was running out.

"Walk me to the door?" he asked.

"Are you really leaving?"

"You sound surprised—or is it disappointed?"

Her head tilted upward another fraction of an inch.

"Hardly." But her face retained the delicate wash of color. "I'm just surprised that you didn't...you know, take anything."

"What makes you think I didn't?"

Her eyes fastened on him and her lips parted. Such kissable lips. They invited a man's possession.

"Did you?"

He tapped her nose. "Just the memory of your kiss."

Kerry looked away as they reached the front door.

"Will you be coming back inside?" the guard asked them.

"Yes," she answered.

"Your boyfriend should have introduced you to the security team," Spencer said as they started down the steps.

A valet appeared before she could respond. "Claim check, folks?"

Spencer pulled the paper from his breast pocket and handed it to the kid, who immediately trotted off. "Won't Hadden wonder where you are?" he asked.

She looked away. "I told him I was going to see you out."

"Strange relationship."

She still wouldn't meet his eyes, staring at her feet instead. A breeze ruffled her hair, sending silky strands in all directions. He caught the subtle scent he was coming to associate with her.

"If you were my woman," he said softly, "I wouldn't let you go off with another man."

She drew in a sharp breath and raised her head, pushing at the tendrils of hair. "Then I guess it's a good thing I'm not your woman. That's a rather chauvinistic attitude in this day and age."

"Yep. I guess it is." He gave in to impulse and touched the incredible silk of one long tress. Nimbly, she stepped out of range, eyes wide.

"You bring out some pretty basic emotions in a man."

Her lips trembled just the slightest bit. "Hardly."

"You know better than that."

He didn't care that they were standing in front of the house where anyone could see them. With the taste of her still fresh in his memory, he found he wanted more. But when he moved toward her again, she raised her hand to ward him off.

"No."

He paused. "You don't want me to kiss you?"

"Not unless you want to double over in pain."

He smiled at the automatic tilt of her chin and the glint in her eyes. "I think we've already played that scene."

"Want an instant replay?"

He stroked her arm and a quiver moved through her. "If you don't want me to kiss you, why are you trembling?"

Her gaze lowered to his chest. "I'm not trembling."

"Kerry, I'm surprised at you. You're lying. To yourself if not to me."

Her face lifted in swift denial. "Someone needs to stick a pin in that ego of yours."

His lips twitched in another bid to smile. "I suppose you have one on hand?"

"Want to find out?"

The valet drove up and Spencer released her slowly, reaching for the bills he had ready in his pocket.

"Maybe another time."

"There isn't going to be another time."

The valet took the money, with thanks. Spencer didn't watch to see where he went. He focused on the graceful woman standing before him.

"Marriage to Hadden would be a mistake," he told her seriously. "He doesn't love you."

"Oh? Now you're an expert on Hadden? Or on love?"

"I have eyes. So does he. And they aren't exclusively for you, Kerry. Is that what you want?"

Her gaze darted around as she backed up a step. "Goodbye, John, or whoever you are. And good luck."

He watched her turn and run back up the steps toward the house. Slowly, he got into his car and started the engine.

There was no choice.

He would have to kidnap her.

4

HE'D EXPECTED TO WAIT for hours, so Spencer nearly missed her light blue sports car when it turned out of the driveway, just minutes later. She was moving well above the speed limit as she passed the spot where he'd pulled over. He hustled to catch up.

Leaving her engagement party this early didn't portend well for the romance. Had Kerry taken his words to heart, or had Hadden witnessed their scene outside and taken umbrage?

Chagrin made Spencer grip the steering wheel more tightly. He had no business playing around with an engaged woman, no matter how she provoked him. He should have kept his attention focused on recovering the painting.

He nearly lost her when she turned onto the highway. Fortunately, he spotted her taillights and caught the on-ramp in time. He refused to dwell on his plan, such as it was. The redhead claimed Hadden would do anything for his fiancée. Spencer hoped that included trading her for one small painting.

The key was to keep Kerry from knowing she was being traded.

She pulled into an expensive Gaithersburg neighborhood. While the houses weren't in the same class as the Summerton estate, each spacious home was nestled on its own acre of land. There were trees for privacy, but not enough to make them easy targets for thieves or mischief-makers—like him.

She left her car in the driveway and entered through a three-car garage. Spencer parked across the street to give himself a clear view of as much of the house as possible, and waited. Eventually, a light went on in an upstairs corner bedroom. The living-room lights stayed on.

Because she wasn't alone in the house?

Or because she was expecting company?

He dismissed an image of Hadden, telling himself this was a family neighborhood. Kerry must live here with her parents. Maybe they were still at the party.

Hopefully, they weren't inside with her.

Spencer studied the residence with particular attention to the corner bedroom. No convenient balcony or handy trees this time—assuming that was her window.

Breaking into Hadden's estate to save his grandmother was one thing. Breaking into a private household to kidnap someone was another matter entirely. If he had the sense of a common housefly, he'd go home and admit defeat.

And his grandmother would be ruined.

Spencer opened the car door and stepped out. The temperature was falling to a seasonable chill, appropriate to three days before the start of October. Spencer rubbed his arms through his suit jacket and stared at the house. The recent mild weather had lulled everyone into believing fall wasn't real yet.

Sort of like what he was trying to do in his head. He wasn't *really* going to kidnap Kerry.

As he crossed the street, he paused to scoop up a handful of small stones from beneath the rural mailbox. Idly, he wondered if her father was a gun collector.

Spencer strolled across the thick carpet of grass, debating how fast and in which direction to run if the bedroom window didn't belong to her.

Tossing a small stone up and down in his hand, he considered the distance from the front lawn to the window and decided he was certifiable. This was foolish. One of her neighbors would spot him and call the police.

Before he could change his mind, he took aim and lobbed the stone. It struck the wall next to the window and rolled down the side of the house to land in the gutter with a surprisingly loud clatter. Spencer froze.

Nothing else happened.

His second stone pinged at the glass and bounced away to land in the grass.

Still no reaction from inside.

His next shot missed completely. Why the hell didn't he just ring the front doorbell? Mulling that over in his mind, he lobbed another stone. The stone pinged against the glass with more force. The windowshade drew back. A face appeared against the glass.

Whoever it was had more hair than her father was apt to.

Spencer tossed a final stone more gently, directly at the face. He held his breath as it bounced harmlessly against the pane. The window was raised abruptly.

"John?" Her voice was hushed but incredulous. "Is that you?"

"Who were you expecting? I'd ask you to let down your hair, but I don't think it's long enough for me to climb."

"Are you crazy? What are you doing here? How did you find out where I live?"

"My car's across the street." He pointed the direction. "Please come down. It's important." He turned and started walking.

"No. John? Are you listening to me? You can say what you have to say...John?"

It was a calculated risk, but he was pretty sure curiosity would bring her outside.

Once again, he considered telling her the truth, but he couldn't risk even one person knowing something that might cause his grandmother untold embarrassment. If the media got wind of the story they would have a field day.

Minutes later, Kerry stepped from the garage and hurried down the driveway toward the street. Now dressed in jeans and a sweatshirt, she slowed as she approached the car, showing at least a modicum of sense. He turned on the overhead light and waited.

More confidently, she strode to the passenger side and flung open the door. "What are you doing here?"

"We have a problem," he told her. "The police know we broke in tonight. They've got warrants for our arrest."

"What?"

"Get in."

His calm certainty had the desired effect. She slid inside. "Is this a joke?"

"Do I look like I'm joking?"

Her face went paper-white. Guilt speared his conscience. He had to remind himself he was doing this for his grandmother.

"What are we going to do?" she asked.

Spencer started the car. "First, we need to get out of here before the police arrive."

"Wait! I can't leave. I—"

He pulled away from the curb. Headlights turned in at the bottom of the street behind them. Spencer used them to his advantage.

"They're coming," he told her.

Her head whipped around. The other car was far

enough away that he was pretty sure she wouldn't be able to see more than oncoming headlights.

"Get down," he ordered.

Miraculously, she obeyed.

"They don't know who I am or what I'm driving, so I won't get stopped. You're the one they've identified. You and your mysterious friend, John."

She groaned. "This can't be happening!"

"That's the truth," he muttered, feeling guiltier by the minute.

"I don't even have my purse with me."

"Don't worry about it. They won't let you have a purse in jail."

"Jail! But we didn't do anything."

"Except break into the bedroom and the safe."

"But we didn't take..." Her head whipped up to stare at him. "Oh, my God, you didn't. You said you didn't take anything."

Spencer blinked in surprise. "I didn't."

"You must have. Why else would the police care?"

"Calm down."

"Calm down! We're going to jail and you want me to calm down?"

"We aren't going to jail. That's why I came and got you. I figured you just needed a little time to explain things to Hadden."

She buried her face in her hands. "Tell me the truth. What did you take? The jewelry or the money?"

About to protest his innocence, Spencer quickly shut up. Lying was bad enough. He wasn't about to start explaining his lies.

"Look, I know a cabin by the lake that's empty. We'll head there until I can set up a meeting with Hadden."

"What lake? And why do you need to meet with Hadden?"

"It's a small resort lake just over the state line in Pennsylvania. What happened with you and Hadden? Did you two have a fight? Is that why you left the party early?"

If Hadden was furious with her there went any chance to make a trade.

She was staring at him as if he'd taken leave of his senses. A distinct possibility.

"Of course we didn't fight. I have a headache."

It was his turn to groan.

"Give me what you stole and take me back to the estate," she demanded. "I'll talk to him."

"You'd never get near him with the police there," he argued. "Let me call and arrange to meet him."

She shook her head and hair whipped across her face. She shoved it back with an unsteady hand. "I don't believe this. I simply don't believe this."

"Welcome to the world of felony B and E."

"My grandfather is going to kill me."

He thought about what his own grandmother would say and cringed. "Not your parents?"

That brought her head back up. "Leave my parents out of this. I don't live with my parents."

"But you live with your grandfather?" He turned off the highway.

"Of course not. It's none of your business who I live with. Take me back to my grandfather's. I can't leave him there alone to face the police."

"I can't do that." He accelerated, telling himself there was no turning back.

"Of course you can. I can make them see reason."

"What about my parole officer? Can you make him see reason too?"

He heard her draw in a sharp breath and wondered where his words had come from. He was digging himself in deeper and deeper. She was going to kill him when she learned the truth.

"You're on parole?"

Spencer shrugged. "What can I say? This time they'll lock me up and throw away the key."

"Why? Why do you take such risks? Surely you could make a living doing something else."

He thought about the prestigious engineering firm he worked for. Staid, workaholic engineers did not build solid careers pretending to be felons. Taylor Engineering was not going to be happy if any of these events surfaced. Already he regretted these lies and his foolish actions.

"I'll leave you out of everything," she said quickly. She laid her hand on his forearm in a gesture of comfort. That only made him feel worse.

"Your friend saw me, remember? She knows you weren't alone in that bedroom," he reminded her.

"Oh, God. What are we going to do?"

Good question. Her fear was starting to etch a spot in his stomach.

"Look, I'll call Hadden and ask for a meeting," he told her. "I'll tell him I kidnapped you—threatened you."

"You can't do that!"

"Sure I can. Don't worry, it will all work out."

She lapsed into silence as the night rushed past them. Privately, Spencer wondered when he'd taken leave of his senses. Hadden seemed more devoted to the redhead than to Kerry. Would Hadden really trade her for the painting? Or would he simply call the cops for real? This had been a really dumb idea.

Spencer looked down at her left hand.

"You left before Hadden gave you the ring?"

She jumped and twisted her head away to stare out the window. "I wasn't feeling well," she said softly.

A prickly feeling scaled its way up his back. Something was badly skewed here.

"Was this or was this not your engagement party? Are you having second thoughts?" The idea pleased him enormously.

"Of course not. Hadden understands." She sounded nervous. "Our friends will understand too."

Maybe they would, but Spencer didn't. His conviction that he'd missed something important grew stronger. He pulled into a deserted gas station before they crossed into Pennsylvania. The wind had picked up considerably, tossing leaves across the ground in swirling profusion. In the distance, he thought he saw lightning.

"What are you doing?" she asked.

"I'm going to call Hadden."

"No!"

"Why not?"

"I'll call him."

"Trust me." He reached for the door handle.

"I *don't* think so."

"It'll be okay. Wait here."

She didn't, of course. She jumped from the car and scrambled after him. He closed himself inside the old-fashioned booth while she glared from the other side of the glass. It occurred to him that he didn't know the number. He cracked open the door. "What's Hadden's phone number?"

Her face went blank.

"You don't know his phone number?"

She looked away. "I'm not going to tell you."

Spencer sighed. He closed the door and pulled open the telephone book as the booth shuddered beneath the onslaught of a gust of wind. Unbelievably, the phone number was listed.

A servant answered. He was certain Hadden III couldn't be disturbed.

"Look, this is important," Spencer protested.

"I'm sorry, sir, but he has guests—" Apparently, the party was still going strong.

"Tell him it's an emergency."

Kerry watched with strained features, her fingers curling and uncurling at her sides.

After a pause, the voice on the other end said, "Just a moment," and the receiver clattered against a hard surface.

The pause grew until Spencer was about to lose his nerve and hang up. Suddenly, a new voice filled his ear.

"Summerton."

Spencer took a deep breath. "About time. I have your fiancée. We need to make a trade."

Another pause.

"Who is this?"

Spencer gripped the phone more tightly. "I told you. The man who has your fiancée."

A chortle sounded in his ear. "Arthur? Is that you? You clown. When did you get back into town?"

"No. This isn't—"

"You almost had me going there for a minute, pal. Look, I've got a house full of guests right now. I'll call you in the morning. We'll meet for lunch. Better yet, come on over. This party should last well into the early hours."

"This is not Arthur!" But he'd lost his audience. A feminine voice was saying something insistent and Hadden was listening to her, not Spencer.

"Sorry, Arthur. I've gotta run. Call you tomorrow."

And the phone disconnected in his ear.

Spencer stood silent in disbelief. Then he fished for

another quarter and redialed. A busy signal buzzed in his ear.

Kerry pounded on the glass. "What happened? What did he say?"

Spencer opened the door and took a deep breath. "He hung up on me."

"What did you say to him?"

"Weren't you listening?" He started back toward the car, glancing at the sky overhead while she kept pace at his side. Unless he missed his guess, a storm was heading right for them.

"I couldn't hear you. You were talking too softly."

Spencer grimaced. "You didn't miss a thing. I told him we needed to make a trade. He thinks I'm someone named Arthur. He's going to call me in the morning so we can do lunch. Arthur is going to be surprised."

"That isn't funny."

"You're telling me."

He opened the car door and she slid inside. Immediately, she twisted toward the driver's seat as she waited for him to get in.

"Now what?" she demanded.

Exhaustion stole over him like the thief he'd pretended to be. It sapped his energy and his ability to think. "Let's go to the cabin. My brain is turning to mush."

"Take me home."

Spencer shook his head. "Not tonight. It'll be all I can do to drive us to the lake."

"I don't want to go to the lake. And I can drive."

"No." He was tempted to chuck the whole silly plan.

"Why not?"

"Look, I'm too tired to argue with you."

"Good. Then let me drive. I am not going to spend

the night with you." Her eyes glittered in the light from the dashboard.

"Afraid?" he asked, knowing darn well she wasn't.

"Yes," she said warningly. "There's always the danger I might give in to the need to choke you to death."

He almost laughed out loud. "Don't worry. There're two bedrooms. I'll lock my door."

"You're insufferable, do you know that?"

"Everybody's got to have a hobby."

HE PULLED INTO the narrow lane leading to the cabin, wondering if he'd left a change of clothing there the last time he'd stayed. He certainly hoped so. Confronting Hadden in a tuxedo tomorrow morning would require explanations he couldn't make.

Headlights illuminated first the lake and then the A-frame building that rose in a majestic splendor of wood and glass. The surrounding woods were darkly sinister, making the location seem more isolated than it really was. Spencer thought he heard a low rumble of thunder in the distance.

"Nice place," she said. "How does a burglar come to own something like this?"

"Who says I own it?"

As he parked, she whirled on him. "Look, buster. Breaking into homes may be your profession, but it isn't mine. We are not going to break in there, do you understand me? You're in enough trouble."

Her aggressive concern amused him, even as it increased his guilt. The lies were starting to bug him.

"It's okay," he told her softly. "The cabin belongs to my grandmother. I have a key and everything."

"Oh." She looked from him to the house and back again. "But I want to go home."

He thought of his apartment and the king-size bed

that waited there. "Me too, but this is safer. It's just for tonight, I promise."

She looked momentarily defeated. Spencer hated that look. He knew one sure way to banish it. At least that's what he told himself as he leaned across the seat, giving her time to realize his intent.

He ignored the prick of conscience that told him not to do this. The memory of her lips on his was no match for his internal objections. Just one more time, he needed to taste her. She was like a drug in his system. He needed more.

In the darkness, her eyes were wide and watchful but she didn't pull away. That was all the encouragement he needed. Spencer sought her lips with his own.

Brenna knew this was wrong. She should pull away. Instead, she clung to his shoulders while he fitted himself to the contour of her mouth. This wasn't the hard, demanding kiss from Hadden's bedroom. This was a teasing brushfire building slowly. The subtle assault on her senses was all the more powerful because there was no demand. Only gentle, incredible persuasion.

Resistance was out of the question the moment that he touched her. When his arms encircled her, drawing her against his chest, coherent thoughts drifted away on the evening air.

His mouth stirred a response that threatened to become a raging firestorm. She heard a restless moan, shocked to realize it had sprung from low in her own throat.

His hands stroked her back with a sure masculine touch and his tongue teased, flitting back and forth, bidding her lips to part. Brenna responded, a searing heat stunning her as his tongue probed for entrance.

Hot, erotic need melted her senses. She arched in pleasure, lost in a multitude of sensations. One of his hands threaded through her hair, cupping the back of her head to anchor her gently, firmly in his arms. It was such a strangely proprietary sensation, yet incredibly sensual.

What his mouth was doing to her went well beyond mere kissing. She was being possessed. And loving it.

Brenna clung to his shoulders and kissed him back, finding the slight rasp of his light stubble against her skin even more arousing. She savored the taste and scent of him, shivering beneath the delicious wave of sensations rolling inside her.

Gently, his teeth nibbled on her bottom lip. Brenna gasped. Spencer attempted to gather her more tightly against his chest, and his elbow thwacked into the steering column.

"Damn!"

He pulled back, leaving her disoriented and paralyzed by the intensity of the need he'd created within her.

"Come on. We'll finish this inside."

His husky words, combined with the sudden wash of chilled air, brought her out of the sensual haze with startling abruptness.

Brenna sank back against her seat. "No." Her mouth throbbed in tandem with the wild beating of her heart. "We can't do this."

"I assure you, we can." His smile was crooked. "But not here."

Sanity returned with a shake of her head. "I don't believe this."

"Me either." He pushed his glasses back against the bridge of his nose, running a hand through his hair. Only then did she realize he was as affected as she was by the kiss. The knowledge was strangely comforting.

"I didn't mean to do that," he said softly.

"You'd better take me home."

"No, I—"

"Now." She forced her fingers to unclench before the nails drew blood in the palms of her hands. She still wanted him. The heady thought was terrifying. "I don't care how sexy you are, I am not going to sleep with you."

His eyes glinted in the darkness. "You think I'm sexy?"

How dare he tease her?

He held up his hands, palms facing her. "Okay, okay." A devilish smile stole across his face. "We wouldn't get much sleep anyhow if we got in the same bed. And I did promise you a separate room."

"I want to go home."

"First thing in the morning. Okay?"

"No."

"Look, can't we give everyone a few hours to calm down? In the morning, we'll talk to Hadden and explain. He'll call off the police, you can go back home, and I'll disappear from your life forever. Deal?"

A strange mix of emotions stirred in her chest. Brenna studied his earnest expression. She wanted to go back to her grandfather's place, but she didn't want the police to arrest this man even if he was a thief. And for some stupid, unfathomable reason, she didn't want him to disappear from her life.

"I must be crazy."

"I know the feeling," he muttered. "Here."

He pulled the car keys from the ignition and handed them to her.

"If you really feel up to driving yourself home tonight, go ahead. I'm beat and I'm going to bed. Try not to tell the police where I am before morning, okay? The cots in jail are really disgusting to sleep on."

He stepped from the car.

Why did she feel as if she was being conned?

Brenna clutched the keys and debated her options. Common sense told her to get behind the wheel and take off. Hormones told her to give him a chance.

He never once looked back as he climbed the front porch steps.

She fingered the keys in her hand. Darn it. She didn't want to be responsible for sending him back to jail even if he was a thief. He seemed intelligent and educated. Why did he have to steal? For thrills? Or was there another, more important reason behind his actions?

Brenna accepted the fact that she was going to do something totally stupid. She opened the car door and stepped into the chilly night air. He turned to watch her hurry across the grass.

"I'm glad you changed your mind," he said quietly.

"I *must* be crazy." She shivered, and not entirely from the damp cold wind. He had a way of looking at her that started all sorts of wicked, wanton thoughts skittering through her mind.

He reached as though for the keys, but took her hand instead. His fingers lightly traced her skin causing another shiver of desire. Brenna had never felt such a connection to another person before. He was seducing her without a word.

Unbidden, her other hand came to rest against his tuxedo jacket. She felt the rise and fall of his chest beneath her fingers. His eyes glimmered mysteriously in the moonlight as they watched her from behind the lenses of his glasses.

"I don't think you're crazy at all," he told her. "I think you're beautiful."

Her breath caught in the back of her throat. Slowly, giving her time to pull away, he bent his head and captured her lips.

The kiss was soft. A tender kiss that left her knees

weak and her body shaking. She gripped his arms for support, swaying against the hard length of him.

"What are you doing to me?" she asked.

"Not nearly as much as I'd like."

She dropped her hands and stepped back.

"This is...I can't...you..."

"It's okay, Kerry. I won't force myself on you."

Kerry. He still thought she was Kerry.

Brenna took a deep breath and struggled for control. "I'm not..."

A gust of cold wind swept across the lake, accompanied by a low rumble of thunder. Oh, God, it wasn't going to rain, was it? Goose bumps rose along her arms as she turned to stare at the black sky.

"May I have the keys?" he asked.

"What?"

"The house key is on that ring."

"Oh." She handed him the keys, careful not to touch him this time. Touching him was dangerous—worse than any storm.

"How did you plan to get inside if I left with your car?"

A naughty grin crossed his face.

"Never mind. Stupid question to ask a burglar. Can we get inside before I freeze?"

"Good idea."

He unlocked the door. A moment later, soft lights revealed a lovely open floor plan with huge windows that stretched to the ceiling along the wall overlooking the water. An enormous brick fireplace covered most of one wall, an inviting, multihued sectional sofa curled before it.

"Oh."

"Yeah. Pretty spectacular, isn't it? Grandma knows how to achieve an effect. Let me get a fire going and turn up the heat a little."

His voice was low. Husky. His gaze captured hers. She found her breath stuck in her chest, waiting for the tingles of awareness to stop.

"You are talking about the fireplace, aren't you?" Was that shaky little voice really hers?

His eyes swept her, leaving warmth in their wake. "Yeah. That too."

5

"THE BEDROOMS ARE upstairs?" she asked. His eyes never left hers. They smoldered darkly behind the lenses of his glasses. Okay, maybe she was the one doing the smoldering. He was so appealing, and he knew it, darn the man.

"Uh-huh," he agreed.

Brenna had to clear her throat. Somehow, she couldn't look away. "There aren't any doors."

"I know."

He watched and waited.

Brenna frowned. "You said I could lock my door."

"And you could, if there was one to lock." His slow smile was pure sin. "Do you think you'll need a lock?"

Oh, yes. Because he was entirely too tempting. Hormones weren't supposed to dance like this.

"I'm not afraid of you," she managed.

"Well, you terrify me."

That stopped her musing.

"You distract me, Kerry," he said seriously. "I can't afford to be distracted right now."

The low thrum of his voice reminded her of a cat's purr. A very large tomcat. And Brenna had to resist an urge to arch her back in coy surrender. She'd never been more aware that she was female.

"Actually," he said softly, "there are doors on the closets and the bathrooms. There's even a connecting door between the two bedrooms. You can lock that...if you want to."

She swallowed and raised her eyes to the loft overhead. Two stairways led up, one on either side of the vast open great room. There were strong support columns for the loft area, she noticed, but they hardly disturbed the sense of airy openness. She had to look close to see the narrow wall that ran between the upper sleeping areas giving an illusion of privacy. From down here she couldn't see the beds.

"Why don't you take the master bedroom on the right?" He tipped his head to one side and gave an exaggerated leer. "Unless you want to share?"

Oh, yeah, with every fiber of her femininity, she yearned to share with him. His kisses had tempted her beyond reason. But he was a thief, and unless she also wanted to share matching jail cells, there was no place for their peculiar relationship to go.

They had nothing in common. They even lived hundreds of miles apart. Getting involved with this man could only lead to heartbreak for her. Still, for one magic night, would it hurt to taste the forbidden?

Sanity prevailed. Brenna shook her head. "I'll take the bedroom on the right."

For a second, she almost changed her mind. Then he banked the smoldering invitation his body had been sending hers and smiled, an openly boyish grin that touched yet another chord within her.

"Okay, but if you change your mind..."

"I won't." Brenna shivered and rubbed her forearms. "You did say this place had heat?"

"I'll turn up the thermostat, but I think it's a little late for a fire. Do you want me to look and see if I have something for you to wear to bed?"

"My clothes will be just fine. We won't be here long, right?"

Again his expression changed. Guilt? She couldn't tell because the expression was gone in an instant. He tilted his head. "You'll be home before your grandfather even knows you're gone."

That reminded her. "I should call him. He'll be worried."

"Does he know you left the house?"

"No. At least he didn't until the police came."

"Sorry." And he really did look sorry. "I should have had you call him from the gas station."

Definitely guilt on that handsome face.

"The phone here has already been disconnected for the winter," he added looking uncomfortable.

"We don't have a telephone? My grandfather will be worried."

"I'm sorry, Kerry."

"Look, it's time for you to know—"

A crash of thunder scattered her words, making both of them jump. Her gaze flew to the wall of glass. Lightning spiked the sky, illuminating the wave-tossed lake.

"It's storming!"

"You aren't afraid of storms, are you?"

"No," she lied.

"Just checking. If you get scared, I'll be happy to let you share a bed with me."

She knew he was teasing. Good thing he didn't know how tempting that offer sounded. "That won't be necessary."

"Darn. Well, I'll go turn up the thermostat. Do you need anything? Something to drink…?"

"No."

"Okay. Sleep well."

Not likely. Nervously, Brenna watched lightning skate across the heavens and wondered which threat was more dangerous—the storm outside or the man who created an entirely different sort of storm inside her. Either way, she probably wouldn't close her eyes all night.

Spencer kept his gaze from following her progress to the room overhead. She was making him crazy. Why the heck couldn't she be unattached?

Of course, she wasn't married yet, but he had never poached—at least, not until now. He knew he was doing something pretty close to that with Kerry, but wasn't his conscience telling him it had to stop? Besides, she obviously wanted commitment. He wasn't in the market for a wife just yet. That's why he dated so many different women. There was safety in numbers, he'd discovered. No one became proprietary when they knew they weren't exclusive. With his career just starting to take off, he didn't have time for the demands of a wife right now.

He checked out the cabin, turned on the hot water tank and adjusted the furnace. The last seemed ridiculous. He was already warmer than he wanted to be and it was all her fault. He should go outside and stand in the rain to cool off.

Instead, he turned off the lights and climbed the left staircase as thunder rumbled overhead. He'd spent many childhood summers here, and the cabin was as familiar as his own apartment. He tugged off his clothes and draped them carelessly before falling into his favorite double bed, one of three that dominated the dormitory-style room. The seriously underinflated waterbed churned beneath him. He hoped the poor old thing would hold together. His grandmother intended to replace it this year, before one of the patches gave out or it sprang another leak.

There was silence on the other side of the wall. Kerry must have gone right to sleep. Spencer wished he could do the same, but his memory kept probing the sweetness of her kisses. He could still feel her body pressed against his. The memory caused a reaction that wasn't conducive to sleep. At this rate, he'd be awake all night.

The room lit with sudden ghostly brilliance, and a large crash shook the house to its foundations, rattling the bank of windows. Kerry cried out. He didn't blame her. That had been a little too close. Seconds later, the connecting door burst open.

"I think the lighting hit something nearby," she exclaimed shrilly.

Spencer sat up. The bed rocked beneath him setting up little waves of motion. Another lightning strike illuminated the room, giving him a momentary view of her.

Her glorious dark hair tumbled wild and invitingly about her shoulders. While she still wore the sweatshirt, she'd taken off the slacks and her long slender legs caused his mind to wander, summoning up a vision of them wrapped around his body.

This was not good. He was becoming obsessive about another man's woman.

"Come here," he said. He should have cleared his throat first. And maybe his vision. He couldn't shake the provocative image she'd evoked.

She crossed the floor, skirting a normal double bed, to stand over him. She trembled, he noticed, as more lightning lit the room.

Passion took a back seat when he realized she was really nervous. "Hey, it's okay. Sit here."

He scooted over and patted the top of the covers.

"I don't think so. I shouldn't have come in here. I just thought a tree or something fell and hit the house." She twisted her fingers together, staring out toward the dark bank of windows that overlooked the lake.

"One might have fallen, but I don't think it hit the

house," he assured her. "Besides, there isn't much we could do about it right now. Are all these windows spooking you?"

"N...no."

"Sit down. I won't leap on you. We might as well watch the fireworks together. I doubt if either of us will get any sleep until they're over."

"I hate storms," she admitted.

"I can tell," he agreed smoothly, inching closer.

She perched on the thin edge of the wooden frame that contained the mattress and popped up in surprise. "Your bed's moving!"

"Waterbeds do that."

She stared at the undulating blanket. "I've never been on a waterbed."

"Here." He patted the sheet next to him. "Lie down and test it out." He tried not to wonder what she was wearing under that sweatshirt.

"No," she said reluctantly.

"Hey, I promise I'm not going to jump on you." And he wouldn't, despite the compelling temptation she presented.

"I *know* you won't." Her tone implied she'd clobber him if he even thought of trying anything.

Spencer grinned. "Come on. You're as safe with me as you want to be. Try it out. The bed is old, but it's still a lot of fun."

She perched awkwardly on the edge. Another crash made her jump. She scooted back just far enough to lose her balance. With a cry of surprise, she toppled backward, landing in the bed with enough force to set up a rolling motion that matched the waters outside. Long strands of her dark hair fell over his face and chest. She landed half on top of him and the tangy scent of her shampoo tickled his nose.

She scrambled away violently. The waterbed rocked in response.

"Take it easy." Spencer reached out and lightly pressed her shoulder into the sheet. "Just lie still a minute. Too much movement and we might spring another leak in this old bed."

"Another leak?" she squeaked.

"Hey, it'll be okay. There. See how the bed's settling?" He wished his body would do the same. Touching her, feeling her body nestled against his, was more unsettling than any waves created by the waterbed.

"I need to get up."

That certainly wasn't his problem. "Okay. Just wait a minute for the bed to calm down."

"Couldn't you have regular beds?" she scolded. "Regular beds don't need to calm down. Regular beds hold still."

Spencer chuckled. "But regular beds aren't as appealing to young children after they've been playing outside in the water all day. Grandma put in the waterbeds to convince us to go to bed and settle down at night when we were young. Going to sleep on a water bed was an adventure."

"Is that what you call this?"

He laughed at her sarcastic tone. "See how the bed is calming?"

"Great. Calm is good. Now how do I get out of this thing?"

She twisted to the side and the bed responded wildly.

"You're struggling again," he told her when she landed fully against his length. Spencer was glad of the sheet and blanket that covered his reaction to her proximity.

"I'm trapped!"

He wished. "You aren't trapped. Easy. Slow, gentle movements."

"This isn't funny!"

"I'd have to disagree."

She stopped moving and glared at him in the darkness. She barely started at the next burst of thunder.

"Just hold completely still for a minute," he offered. "This is a really old waterbed. The newer ones don't rock like this."

"Wonderful. I wonder how many people have died trying to escape the clutches of old water beds."

He smiled as he pressed her shoulder into stillness again. She had a very nice shoulder. Heck, she had a nice everything and he wasn't supposed to be noticing that.

"There. See? The waves are slowing down."

Lightning flamed, starkly revealing her expression in its wake. Her face was only inches from his. She had the most compelling eyes, he decided.

"Are you going to help me get out of this thing?"

Her shaky words cut through the building sensual haze.

"If you insist."

"I do."

"I was afraid of that. You know, my grandmother used to sit with us at night and tell us stories when it stormed. Exciting stories to match the clash of the thunder."

She quickly scooted backward setting up another swaying motion. "You're planning to tell me stories?" she asked with a trace of humor.

Spencer maneuvered closer. "I could. Would you like me to?"

"I don't think so." She tossed back a strand of hair. "Somehow, I don't think your stories would have the same effect."

"Probably not." He touched her arm before he could stop himself. Her body tensed in reaction. So did his. He rubbed the sweatshirt lightly. The bed swished beneath them. She focused on his hand. She didn't seem to notice the next clash of thunder at all.

"I'd better get up," she said softly.

"Okay."

Another dazzling streak of lightning, immediately followed by a loud clap of thunder, sent her scrambling again. The bed reacted violently. They landed back in the center once more.

"Good grief," she muttered.

"Hey, I told you, you have to move slowly. I'm not kidding about a leak. After years of kids bouncing up and down, I don't trust these old seams."

"Great." She stared at his hand where it cushioned her arm. "You want to let go of me now?"

"Not really." But he released her slowly.

They stared at each other in the darkness. Spencer saw the memory of their kiss reflected in the confusion of her thoughts. He knew the feeling.

He kept remembering how sweet she tasted, how good she smelled, how responsive she was. Her small moans of contentment had tightened his arousal until he nearly forgot himself completely in the incredible desire to plunge inside her, laying claim to this captivating woman.

"What are you thinking?" she asked.

"I'm thinking that what I really want to do is kiss you again," he told her honestly.

"That's a terrible idea."

She sounded breathless. His own breath felt trapped in his chest. Normally, Spencer enjoyed the art of seduction. Seducing and being seduced were pleasurable activities with the right person. But with Brenna, the situation was clouded by the fact that he couldn't be sure which of them was doing the seducing and which was being seduced.

"Yeah. A terrible idea," he muttered.

She didn't withdraw as he leaned close enough for her to hear the rapid beating of his heart. The lightning's sizzle took a back seat to the tension arcing between them. He was already hard as his body clamored with the need to touch her.

Slowly, his hand rose to trace the curve of her chin. She went completely still. Her lips parted. He wondered if she knew her fingernails were biting into the bare skin of his arm.

He followed the satin curve of her jaw with a fingertip, moving down until he came to the pulse point beating a frantic cadence in her throat. She trembled delicately, watching him from eyes that appeared luminous in the darkness of the room.

Lightning flared again briefly. The waterbed gently nudged their bodies together. Silently, he blessed his grandmother for never replacing this old bed with a newer, more stable version.

"This…isn't…a good idea," she said with a ragged catch to her voice.

"Oh, I know that."

Her pulse rate increased, sending his skyrocketing. Touching wasn't enough. The need to thrust himself deep inside her welcoming body rose like a molten river. Hot, liquid, unstoppable.

"I'm full of bad and wild ideas right now."

"Like what?"

The whispered question destroyed his good intentions. He cupped the side of her face with his palm. She quivered. Or maybe that was the bed. It could even have been him. Brenna was driving him right over the edge and she hadn't even touched him, yet.

But, oh, how he craved that touch.

He closed the inches that separated them, holding her face still with both hands as the water undulated beneath them and thunder echoed in the sky overhead.

Initially, he'd only meant to offer comfort. Now, he felt as though he stood at the edge of a precipice. Spencer knew how to master his emotions and his actions. No woman had ever pushed him beyond the limits of his control.

Until now.

He should have known their attraction was too strong. He'd wanted to claim her from the first moment he felt her body squirming beneath his on Hadden's bedroom floor.

"You're like the storm," he told her softly, "filled with raw excitement."

She gazed at him and her trembling increased. But, lightning illuminated the hint of a smile that played at the corners of her mouth—such a warm, kissable mouth.

"Does that line work very often?" she asked.

He wanted to laugh at her ability to read him so clearly. "I don't know. I've never used it before."

The bed pushed their bodies even closer. She bumped gently against him. The motion was sensual, sexual, arousing.

"I think you'd better tell me to stop," he warned. His fingers stroked her cheek. She had the softest skin. Just like her lips.

"Stop?"

Her hesitant question gave him all the incentive he needed.

"Too late."

He covered her lips, and they were every bit as honeyed and supple as he remembered. A thrill shot through him as her lips eagerly clung to his.

He stroked her arms and her back, resenting the barrier of her sweatshirt. He wanted nothing between them but a sheen of mutual passion. Spencer wanted to feel her body bared and pressed against his own.

The bed churned beneath them.

Her hands gripped his shoulders, alternately rubbing back and forth over the taut skin of his back. An unconscious scrape of nail caused his muscles to contract. He lifted her chin to nibble along the delicate flesh of her neck.

She made a low sound and trembled violently. And not because of the receding storm. He only noticed the next flash of light because it gave him a moment to see her expression.

Brenna's eyes were closed, her lips parted sensuously as her necked curved up and back to allow him access to the sensitive skin. A small moan of pleasure escaped, driving all traces of his sanity right out the window.

Spencer slid his hands down her sides, passing lightly over the sides of her breasts. Such perfectly molded breasts. They were made to be cupped and fondled. And they fit so snugly against his palms. She made another small sound, teasing him with the tip of her tongue.

He'd never felt so hot, so completely out of control. He pinched the tiny nub of her nipple through the material of her sweatshirt and she moaned into his mouth.

The bed beneath them rocked harder.

He should stop. He knew he should stop.

His hands slid beneath the sweatshirt to stroke her silken body, to explore the lissome strength of her. Lightning split the sky. The room rocked beneath a new blast of thunder. He barely noticed.

Her nipple was pressed against his palm. Her body writhed in satisfaction beneath his touch.

The waterbed writhed as well.

He had to stop now. But his body had a mind of its own. All thoughts of control were driven away by the storm raging inside him as her tongue suddenly flicked out to lick at the curve of his neck.

His hand slid across the plane of her stomach, down across her panties, finding the dampness that waited at the apex of her thighs. She curved upward, straining toward his touch.

Spencer smiled and slid a finger beneath the thin elastic. She gave another soft cry and opened her legs to give him better access. Her hands gripped, then stroked his skin in maddening delight. And every place she touched left prickles of sensitized skin in its wake. He brushed his hand across the wiry curls guarding her femininity. She quivered in delight and her tongue suddenly flicked out to lick at the curve of his neck.

"You're driving me crazy," he whispered.

"Yes!"

The bed rolled in tandem to the urgency rocking her against his hand. She was so incredibly responsive. His other hand encircled her bared breast. The nipple strained against his palm. He slid one finger inside her warmth as he lowered his head to her breast.

Brenna's soft, passionate cry nearly undid him then and there. Spencer sucked strongly. She pressed herself against him as thunder boomed overhead.

The bed rocked as well.

Her fingers sought the pulsing hunger of his erection. He withdrew his hand to move against her, pausing to kiss her neck, sucking at the tender skin.

"Oh, my!" she cried.

Her body bowed against his, fitting snugly. Even as

he gloried in her freely given response, his body clamored for more. He tugged on her bared nipple and realized he had no control left at all. He needed to be inside her.

Right now!

Water, wet and cold, soaked his shoulder.

Spencer drew back with a hoarse cry of surprise. The bed swished violently. Water saturated the sheets.

"Oh!" Kerry gasped in dismay. She stared at him blankly, the look of passion fading beneath an expression of shocked disbelief. He knew just how she felt.

He pulled away. More water flowed across his bare skin.

"Damn it! I don't believe this! We *did* spring a leak!"

Brenna scrambled, trying to get away from the cold wetness permeating her side and now her back. Thunder mocked her attempts to climb from the bed as the water swished from side to side with Spencer's efforts to get free of the sheets.

"Would you hold still?" she demanded. "We're going to drown."

"We're not going to drown. Damn, this water's cold."

"I noticed." Brenna managed to climb over the wooden frame and stood dripping on the polished hardwood floor. She shivered, but she knew the shiver was due to more than the cold wetness of the bed. It was like being jarred awake from a sensual dream that had engulfed her mind and body.

What had she been doing? She didn't want to want this man. Brenna had never gone in for casual affairs or brief flings like some of her acquaintances. Sex was too personal. Too important to share with just anyone.

Lightning flickered at the windows. The man she'd almost made love with was cursing, groping on the nightstand for his glasses. Water continued to rise inside the frame, saturating him and the linens. He finally clambered from the bed and she saw he was totally, magnificently nude and still partially aroused.

"Don't just stand there," he commanded. "Grab some towels from the bathroom. If we ruin the floors, Grandma will kill me."

Brenna couldn't help it, she began to giggle, partly in release. But the idea of this incredible male specimen being afraid of his grandmother, after all that had happened, struck her as funny.

He strode in her direction. "I am going to assume you are laughing at the situation," he said with quiet intensity.

"What else...? Oh." And another giggle bubbled up. In the dark, he loomed shadowy and dangerous. A warrior of old.

"That does it. One more giggle and I'm going to paddle you, as soon as we get this mess cleaned up."

"Oh? So you're into that, are you?" As soon as the outrageous words left her mouth, Brenna opted for caution. She stepped toward what she hoped was the bathroom door. "I don't do kinky sex," she added, and darted inside.

She was stunned by her boldness. Even more so by what she'd almost committed to on the bed just now. Two more minutes and she would have begged him to make love to her.

Had she taken complete leave of her senses?

On Sunday, she'd return to her real life in New York City. She couldn't start an affair with a man who lived in Maryland.

What was she thinking? Where he lived didn't make any difference. He was a professional burglar! Because of him she was wanted by the police.

And she'd very nearly made love with him.

Brenna hit the light switch. Nothing happened.

Apparently, the storm had taken down the power lines. She gathered a handful of towels by feel. Should she curse the waterbed, or thank it for the timely rescue? Her burglar was a very well-endowed male. An enormously appealing, enticing male.

She couldn't think about that now. Her wet sweatshirt clung to her bare skin uncomfortably. She set the towels down and started to pull it over her head when she remembered that all she had on were panties and the sweatshirt.

"Great. Just great."

Thunder boomed overhead.

"Oh, be quiet," she muttered, no longer intimidated by the fury of the storm. She had something much more intimidating waiting for her in the bedroom.

She reentered the room to find him dashing up the steps, a garden hose in one hand. He'd not only had time to run downstairs, but also to pull on a pair of shorts, she noticed as he rushed to the window behind the bed and threw it open. Wind drove rain into the room.

"Are you crazy? What are you doing?!"

"We have to drain the bed," he told her. He lifted a garden hose from inside the pooling puddle that was now the inside of the bed. "Help me submerge the other end of the hose. Keep it down and whatever you do, don't let it come out of the water."

Brenna set aside the towels and hurried forward to plunge her hand into the cold liquid, feeling for the other end of the hose. "Where did you get this?"

"We keep one in the mud room downstairs."

Water sloshed to the wet floor. After a few minutes, he lifted his end of the hose and dropped it out the window.

"This will never work," she told him. Rain pelted

them through the partially open window. They might as well have been outside.

"Sure it will. We've done it before. My brother's kid poked a huge hole in this bed a few years ago."

"We were lying on a patched waterbed?"

"It's the only one left. Grandma replaced the other beds with regular mattresses and box springs after my sister brought her cat here. The cat decided to sharpen her claws on the bed." Wryly, he added, "That was one surprised cat. Wait here and don't let go of that hose."

"Where are you going?"

"To find something heavy to set on the hose so it won't come out of the water."

"We could just take turns holding it down."

"All night?"

"No, not all night. Just until the bed is drained."

"Kerry, that's going to take all night. This is a very small garden hose. The larger one is outside in the shed and I don't think outside is where I want to go right now."

Thunder punctuated his assessment.

"My name's not…"

But he was already halfway down the stairs. Brenna held the hose in place and explained to the dying bed about the defective chromosome that held men back on the evolutionary ladder.

"They do have one redeeming feature," she concluded, and then pictured him standing in the darkened room like a gloriously naked gladiator. "Okay, maybe more than one. But sometimes they aren't too bright."

"Who's not too bright?"

She turned to find he'd silently returned. Why didn't he look any less sexy wearing a pair of cut-off shorts than he had in a tux, or totally naked?

"Me. I'm not too bright or I wouldn't be sitting next to a dying bed, sucking water from its innards."

He laughed. "I never quite thought of it like that." He submerged a large metal skillet into the water, careful to keep the nozzle underwater. "That should hold it. Now then, where were we?"

"Wiping water off the floor?" she asked with false sweetness.

"Guess the bed pretty well killed the mood, huh?"

"Not a bad replacement for a cold shower. A bit unexpected, but then, everything about you has been unexpected." She tossed him the towels. "Do have fun."

"Where are you going?"

"Back to my room where it isn't raining on the inside. I think the loud part of the storm is almost past us."

"Hey, you can't be sure of that. It could start thundering again at any moment."

"I'll take my chances. You've helped me put my fear in perspective. Sleep well."

"Don't you think we should talk?"

"About what?"

He nudged his glasses up the bridge of his nose. "You. Me. Hadden. What almost happened."

She averted her eyes from his bare chest and tried not to remember the feel of his skin beneath her fingers.

"It's okay. I forgive you for nearly drowning me. You'd better get some rest tonight. In the morning we're going to have a truly meaningful conversation about what you stole from the estate and how you are going to give up a life of crime."

"Uh, maybe I'd better tell you the truth."

"Count on it, buster, but your hose just fell out of the window."

He looked down. "Damn!" He rushed forward as water began pooling on the floor.

"Sleep tight."

She managed to get through the connecting door before she gave in to any more impulses. She'd nearly made love with a thief, nearly drowned in his grandmother's waterbed, the police were looking for her, Hadden and Kerry were probably ready to murder her, and all she could think about was that the darn stupid waterbed had picked a heck of a time to spring a leak.

In the morning, she was going to straighten out his misconception about her name and talk him into giving himself up.

And tonight, she was going to stay away from her sexy housemate no matter how much her body disagreed.

6

SPENCER WOKE EARLY and shivered. His frosty breath hung in the crisp cold air. The temperature had descended right along with the rain last night. And with an open window and no electricity, he was made well aware of that fact.

He checked the waterbed, repositioned the hose, and mopped up some spills he'd missed in the dark. His Grandmother was not going to be happy. He'd leave Kerry's participation out of the story when he told her what happened.

The cabin was silent. Quietly, he dug through the closet until he turned up a pair of jeans, a shirt and an old sweatshirt to wear. He even found, miraculously, clean socks and underwear in one of the drawers. His entire family used the cabin as a second home. Kerry could just help herself.

He resisted the temptation to open the connecting door and check on her. He did not need to see her looking all soft and rumpled against the sheets. She was enough of an enticement awake and fully dressed.

Since it was later than he'd planned on getting started, Spencer hurried outside. If he was lucky, he could talk to Hadden, get the painting, and be back before she woke.

Now that he'd slept on his ridiculous plan to kidnap her, he saw how totally stupid the whole thing was.

He must have been out of his mind last night. Worry over his grandmother's reputation was no excuse.

Heading back down the interstate, he decided to explain to Hadden—in ambiguous terms—why he needed the painting.

Spencer was still mulling over his options when he turned down the street leading to the Summerton estate. A flashy, hot orange sports car suddenly zipped recklessly from the Summerton driveway. Hadden sat behind the wheel. Spencer's stomach turned to stone. A riot of carroty-red hair nestled against Hadden's shoulder.

As the car passed, Spencer slowed for a better view, even though he knew who the passenger had to be. Sure enough, there sat Kerry's good friend, the redhead from last night. Obviously, she'd just spent the night with Hadden Summerton III. And from the look of things, theirs hadn't been a platonic evening.

Spencer clenched his teeth.

Okay, so maybe Kerry's evening hadn't been completely platonic either, but nothing serious had happened. He refused to dwell on how close that had been. He'd never put moves on another man's woman before and the memory disturbed him.

On the other hand, another man's woman shouldn't have responded to him the way Kerry had. They'd been a water patch away from becoming lovers last night. Kerry struck him as inherently honest and that presented a contradiction he couldn't understand.

Unless she wasn't really Kerry Martin.

So many things would be explained. Including why a supposedly happy bride-to-be could kiss a complete stranger sweetly enough to curl his toes and start him thinking about happily ever after.

Hold it.

He was not thinking about happily ever after here.

He wasn't in the market to be anyone's husband. Even someone as adorable as Kerry. Especially someone like Kerry! They were oil and water. He'd only wanted a fast tumble.

Okay, maybe not fast, and maybe more than a tumble, but the point was, he had no current interest in the state of wedded bliss. Establishing his career came first.

He braked at the closed entrance to the estate. A cleaning service van stood in the turnaround before the front steps. The gate across the entrance itself was locked, but people moved around the grounds. With Hadden out of the way, Spencer could probably talk his way inside.

That miserable painting had to be somewhere.

He eyed the van while his thoughts staggered right back to probing the mystery of Kerry Martin.

If his wild hunch was right, the woman at his grandmother's cabin wasn't really Hadden III's fiancée. He'd found her in Hadden Senior's bedroom. *Under* the bed. What if his original opinion had been the correct one? What if she'd broken in, just as he had?

The thought jelled into a certainty.

He'd just kidnapped someone—and he had no idea who she was.

BRENNA WOKE to bright sunlight, chirping birds and freezing temperatures. Then she remembered the open window. No wonder it was so cold. The power must still be out. No electricity meant no heat. She might as well be sleeping outdoors.

She forced herself up, wrapped an extra blanket around her torso, and hurried to the bathroom. Too late, she remembered there would be no hot water either.

Freezing, from her brief moment under the cold

shower, she rewrapped the blanket and went in search of her sweatshirt. Great. Still too damp to put on. She pulled the blanket around her more tightly.

"John?"

The house was silent. Too silent, she realized. She opened the connecting door. Frigid air greeted her, along with the sight of the rumpled, empty bed nearest the waterbed. A pair of skimpy denim cutoffs lay discarded on the floor.

Brenna shied from the memories of last night. He'd looked far too sexy in those shorts. And even more appealing without them.

Her gaze landed on the waterbed. She was surprised to see that no ice had formed on the water still remaining inside the deflated mattress.

"John?"

The bathroom door and the closet door both gaped open, vacant of human life. Brenna shivered. She walked to the balcony overlooking the great room downstairs and peered over. "John?"

She knew he wasn't going to answer. The house had an abandoned feeling. He'd stolen away while she was sleeping, just like the thief he was.

Brenna fought back a growing sense of panic. How dare he? When she found him, she'd kill him as dead as the waterbed.

She turned back to the closet. A wide variety of clothing hung there. Male clothing mixed with women's attire and even children's outfits. Brenna decided this was no time to be picky. She was freezing. She liberated a long-sleeved white turtleneck and a pretty blue-and-white ski sweater. Yesterday's jeans would do until she could get home to a hot shower and some coffee.

And then it dawned on her. She had no way *to* get

home. Without a phone or a car, she was trapped. Unless her thief came back for her.

Of course he'd come back. He probably went out to get breakfast.

Brenna pulled on her tennis shoes and hurried downstairs, then stopped abruptly halfway down. What if he'd lied to her and broken into this cabin? He could have stolen the key from outside earlier in the day. If that were the case, he wouldn't want to return to the scene of his crime.

Her mind conjured up visions of covering him in honey and staking him over an ant hill—*if* she ever saw him again.

She looked around the empty cabin. Grudgingly, she admitted that the setting was beautiful, quietly rustic and restful. The cabin had a breathtaking view of the lake and forest. The few leaves remaining on the windswept trees wore their scarlet fall plumage with brilliant elegance.

But Brenna did not want to feel tranquil. She was cold and hungry and vastly annoyed as she watched sunlight dapple the water that washed serenely against the pier and small sandy beach. A couple of hardy fishermen sat in boats out in the distance.

Brenna shivered and turned her attention back to the main room. The first order of business was a phone. If John, or whatever his real name was, had lied about the cabin belonging to his grandmother, he might have lied about other things as well.

She started toward the kitchen area beneath the loft, then she noticed another room next to the fireplace. Curious, she headed there first.

Inside was a brightly cheerful home office. It boasted everything from a computer to a fax machine. And, yes, a telephone. She was heading for the sturdy walnut desk when a cluster of paintings caught her eye. The vivid colors, the simplicity of style, told her immediately who the artist had to be. While she'd never seen these particular works before, only her grandfather could have painted the three small canvases.

Brenna moved closer. The tiny B. J. Wolford signature was in the corner of each one. Originals, and older works at that. One was a portrait of a lovely young woman. Since her grandfather rarely did portraits anymore, this painting would be quite valuable. The other two were landscapes, one of them reminiscent of this very lake. Brenna knew her grandfather hadn't painted in this particular style since before she'd been born.

So how did a thief's grandmother come to own such valuable B. J. Wolford originals? Were they stolen?

Nervously, she turned to study a grouping of family pictures hanging on the opposite wall. Her heart beat a little faster. Her thief was there in a number of pictures, bold as brass and twice as sassy.

He'd been an adorable child. A handsome teen. And who were all these other people? He'd mentioned a sister. Maybe a brother. Surely he didn't have two of each, did he? No one had big families anymore.

She thought of the wide array of clothing upstairs and decided maybe his parents did. Her eyes flashed to the white-haired woman beside John's father and mother. Now she knew where he got that impish grin. Come to think of it, the older woman looked oddly familiar.

Good grief, the older woman was the subject of the portrait on the other wall. Her face had hardly changed with time.

Brenna removed the picture and carried the family photo over to the painting. No question about it.

Brenna's grandfather had painted a portrait of the thief's grandmother.

A terrible suspicion began to build. She rehung the picture and studied the rest of them. A much older photograph hung nearby. A familiar photograph. One she'd seen in the shoebox full of pictures that her grandfather kept in his closet.

Two men and a woman gazed at the camera. They were laughing as if someone had just told a joke. Filled with the exuberance of youth, they stood beneath the branches of a wide oak tree. B. J. Wolford. Regina Linnington. Hadden Caldwell Summerton.

Brenna's breath caught in her throat. She had to be standing inside Regina Linnington's cabin. The same Regina Linnington who had posed for the nude painting her grandfather had forged. The same painting that Hadden Senior had sold as a Lispkit original. A painting that had netted the three conspirators a tidy fortune to split three ways and now threatened to destroy her grandfather's career and reputation.

"Oh, my God. This can't be happening."

A faint sound from outside sent her hurrying back to the main room. He'd returned. And not a moment too soon. Her thief had some real explaining to do.

Brenna ran into the main room and stopped so fast she nearly slipped on a throw rug. Through the window, the police car sat like a beacon in the gravel driveway. The officer hadn't seen her yet.

He'd climbed out and was standing looking over the lake toward the fishermen.

"Oh, God. Oh, God."

Her heart pounded. She'd be thrown in jail. Her grandfather would kill her.

Frantically, Brenna looked for another exit. A doorway led off the kitchen.

"Please, let it lead outside. Please, let it lead outside," she prayed as she ran in that direction.

It led to a washer and dryer and an alcove. She sped past the appliances, through the mud room, to reach an outside exit.

"Thank you, God."

She fumbled with the lock and stumbled outside nearly falling over an enormous tree branch that had blown against the house in the night. Ignoring both the branch and the paths, one leading to a shed, and another that rounded the side of the cabin toward the driveway, she plunged toward the woods.

Her tennis shoes sank in mud to her ankles. She ignored the squishy sound and the ooze seeping inside her shoes and ran.

This was stupid. The policeman would see her footprints and follow her easily. She should have stayed put. Should have tried to bluff her way around the burglary.

Oh, sure. That would have been easy.

Branches tore at her hair and whipped at her cheek. She clambered over a small tree that had probably come down last night, snagging the sweater and scratching her ankle.

She was no good at running a bluff. What lie could she come up with for going through Hadden's safe and covering for a professional burglar? They'd lock her up and throw away the key.

She stumbled and nearly fell over some wide branches and another downed tree.

Never mind torture by ant hills. When she got her hands on her friendly thief again she'd wring his blasted neck with her bare hands—her raw, scraped, bleeding bare hands. The man was toast. She'd incinerate him with pure fury.

She stayed parallel with the rutted road leading to

the cabin so as not to get lost. But she was getting a stitch in her side and realized she had no idea what to do once she reached the main road. Had they turned left or right onto this lane last night? Why hadn't she paid more attention?

The sound of a car engine brought her up short. She leaned against the bole of a tree and clutched her side, panting heavily. Not the police car. This car was heading toward the cabin.

Reinforcements?

Brenna decided she didn't care. She was too winded to keep running.

"John's" dark blue coupé appeared around a curve. Without hesitation, Brenna plunged through the trees and brush, rushing into the road wildly waving her arms.

Spencer nearly had a heart attack. His first thought when he caught the motion out of the corner of his eye was that he'd startled a deer. Instinctively, he slowed.

Her cheeks were flushed a ruddy red. She wore his sister Jayne's favorite blue sweater, a tear now gaping at one shoulder. Leaves tangled in her hair and her feet were covered in mud and bits of debris.

What the hell had happened? He'd only been gone a couple of hours.

She raced to the passenger side and threw herself inside. "Turn around. Turn the car around!"

"You have to be kidding. There's no room—"

"Turn the car around!"

He put the engine in reverse. "What's wrong? What happened?"

He had to inch the car back and then forward since the vehicle was longer than the lane was wide. Trees and soft banks lay waiting on either side for him to make a mistake.

"It would be a lot easier if I drove to the cabin and turned around," he told her.

"Fine. You and the policeman can have a nice long chat, right before he takes you away in handcuffs."

"Policeman?" His heart thundered against his rib cage. "There's a policeman at the cabin? What does he want?"

Her expression of disgust was almost comical. She swiped at a strand of hair falling across her face, leaving behind a long smudge of dirt. Spencer decided against mentioning that to her.

"I can't imagine what he's doing there, John. Silly me. I didn't take time to invite him in for tea and conversation. I thought maybe escape was the better part of stupidity. Now, I'm not so sure."

She glared. The woman had a fierce glare.

Guilt assailed him. Well-deserved guilt. His lies had come home to roost. "Uh, listen, Kerry...."

His attention was distracted as he bumped a tree. She never said a word until he finally managed to get the car turned around without getting stuck in the soft dirt on either side.

"Now, you listen, Mr. Burglar. We are going to Hadden's right now. You are going to return everything you took from his grandfather's estate. You are going to apologize. I am going to convince him not to press charges."

He couldn't help it; he chuckled. "You are, huh?"

"Yes, I am, you...you...you thief! And my name's not Kerry!"

He turned left onto the highway as relief coursed through him. She wasn't Kerry!

"Who are you? And what were you doing hiding in Hadden's bedroom?"

She sat back primly. "That isn't any of your business."

"Like hell it isn't. The police are at the cabin."

"Well, whose fault is that? *I* didn't take anything from the estate."

Her scorn cut into him. "I didn't take anything either."

"Right. That's why the nice policeman came to your grandmother's cabin first thing this morning."

He didn't point out that it was nearly noon.

"The police probably came to check on things after the storm," Spencer explained. "The local cops keep an eye on the cabin in the off season. If you'd just answered the door—"

"Oh, no, you don't. This isn't my fault."

"I didn't say it was."

"You said I should have answered the door. And then what, Mr. Know-It-All? What was I supposed to tell the officer when he asked what I was doing there?"

He flashed her an annoyed frown. "You could have told him you were there with me."

"Right. I could have said *John* brought me to the cabin last night while we were running from the police because *John* had just crashed Hadden Summerton's engagement party and stolen who knows what from his estate. But since *I* had nothing to do with it—"

He was *not* going to feel guilty. "I didn't steal anything!"

She continued on, unperturbed by his interruption. "And then, the nice policeman would ask to see some identification. And I'd have to explain that since they don't allow purses in jail cells, *John* wouldn't let me go back inside my grandfather's house to get any identification."

Spencer cringed. She not only had a point, she drove it home with a sledgehammer.

"Spencer," he said softly.

"What?"

"My name's Spencer Griffen."

She twisted on the seat to stare at him. "You're making that up."

Spencer blinked in surprise. "I'm what?"

"Nobody is named Spencer Griffen. You should stick with John."

"I'll have you know my mother named me Spencer after Spencer Tracy, the old movie actor."

"Why?"

"How do I know why? She named all her kids after old movie stars."

The aggravating woman folded her arms primly across her chest. "How many of you are there?"

"What does that have to do with anything?"

"I'm trying to decide if you're telling me the truth."

The car swerved as he glanced at her in surprise. "If I'm telling the truth? What about you? Pretending to be Kerry Martin so I wouldn't know you were a thief too."

"I am *not* a thief. And I never said I was Kerry Martin. You were the one who jumped to that conclusion."

"Well, you certainly didn't do anything to disabuse me of the notion."

"Why should I? I don't go around telling common burglars my name."

"That does it!"

Spencer pulled the car to the side of the highway and threw it into park. His expression should have put the fear of God into her. Instead, she glared right back at him.

"You are the most aggravating, argumentative female I have ever met. Why would I lie to you about my name?"

"You want me to give you a list?" she asked. "As a professional thief, you must lie all the time."

His jaw clenched. "I am not a thief."

"You said you were," she pointed out.

"I lied!"

She sat back looking smug. "I rest my case."

Spencer fought a tremendous urge to take her by her slim shoulders and give her the shaking of her life. She was making him crazy. She'd been making him crazy since she crawled out from under the bed.

"You are making me crazy," he told her.

"Ha! You were born that way. Your mother should have named you after Jack Nicholson in *One Flew over the Cuckoo's Nest*."

His hands reached for her abruptly, but then gripped her with an amazingly gentle hold. He'd intended to shake her, but his hands had other ideas.

Caution entered her expression. Caution, but also a banked excitement. His own excitement stirred to life the moment he touched her. He should have known better.

"I was already born when they made that movie."

"What?"

His heart thudded at the sensual expression on her face. "*One Flew over the Cuckoo's Nest* was made in the seventies," he managed to explain.

"Oh." Her eyes stared at him, boldly daring him.

"You should come with a warning label," he told her. He enfolded her in his arms until he felt her press against his chest. Her face was only inches from his. "You're playing a dangerous game of temptation," he told her softly.

"Not me. I wouldn't know how."

"Oh, you know how all right." He leaned forward and captured her lips with his. Her hands slipped around his neck and she arched against him, yielding sweetly. He kissed her with lingering softness.

She made a tiny, potent sound of satisfaction. Her fingers tangled in his hair, stroking his head with her fingertips.

He cupped her breast through the sweater and Brenna moaned. A growl of contentment rumbled in the back of his throat. Her tongue slipped inside his mouth, stoking the furnace of desire.

He liked her unexpected aggression as she pulled back and began to alternate sharp little nips along his jaw with soothing licks of her tongue.

He squeezed her breast, alternately rubbing and kneading at the firm skin beneath the sweater and turtleneck she wore. He wasn't prepared for the questing of her fingers as her hand descended to his lap, searching and then finding the pulsing length of him.

Her fingers pressed against the shaft and began to caress him. Spencer made a strangled sound at the unexpected pleasure and saw her lips curve in a knowing smile. The fiendish imp. She was out to drive him completely bonkers. No other woman had ever aroused him to fever pitch so quickly.

"If you keep that up," he warned, "I'm going to take you right here. Right now."

Excitement lit her face. "You wouldn't dare."

He slid his hand beneath her clothing, baring the nearest breast. She cried out as his mouth engulfed the engorged skin. Her fingers squeezed his flesh beneath the too-tight jeans, scattering common sense to the fates.

He had to have her. He'd go insane if he couldn't bury himself inside her. He pulled back and guided her fingers to the zipper of his jeans.

She met his gaze, peering at him through half-closed eyes.

"I suppose you want some help?"

Her sultry voice teased as her fingers continued to rub his flesh beneath the denim.

"Yeah." His voice felt thick, clotted with desire. "Pull it down."

Very slowly, teasing him with her eyes and a smile of womanly power, she kissed him with parted lips as her fingers began to draw the zipper down.

Spencer tugged her against him, desperate for the feel of her hand on his skin.

A double blast from an air horn made them both jump apart. The wake from the truck passing them rocked the small car from side to side.

Spencer cursed. His body was rigid with desire. He couldn't believe he was ready to take her right there on the side of the road in full view of anyone and everyone passing by. She'd made him worse than foolish. He was squirrel fodder—completely nuts.

"Kerry, I'm sorry." He stared straight ahead, gripping the steering wheel.

"Brenna."

He whipped his head around to stare at her. Her puffy lips curved.

"That's your real name?"

"Of course," she said smugly. "*I* haven't lied to *you*."

She was the most desirable, yet the most maddening female he'd ever encountered. "Unless we count omissions."

"What omissions?"

"You let me think you were Kerry Martin."

She straightened his sister's sweater and plucked a brittle yellow leaf from the arm. "I just didn't correct your mistaken impression."

"Why not?"

"Because who I am is none of your business."

He should have shaken her. "The hell it isn't. I kidnapped you because I thought you were engaged to Summerton."

"Kidnapped?" She jerked erect against the seat, fire flashing in her eyes. "What do you mean, you kidnapped me?"

Oops! "Never mind." He put the car in gear and pulled back onto the road.

"Oh, no, you don't. Explain yourself."

"Put your seat belt on."

She drew the belt across her chest with short choppy movements.

"Now explain. What do you mean, you kidnapped me?" she demanded.

A multitude of possible responses flashed through his mind and were discarded just as quickly. No more lies. On the other hand, he couldn't tell her the truth.

"Well, I had to steal something. I chose you."

Her silence nearly suffocated him. Spencer wondered what she was thinking. He darted a glance in her direction, but she was staring straight ahead, her hands twisted in her lap.

"Aren't you going to say something?"

He felt her turn her head to look at him. "I have a great deal to say to you, Spencer Griffen, or whoever you *really* are. But none of it is appropriate while you are driving this car."

Damn, but he liked her. Really liked her. She had more spunk than his two bratty sisters, his mother and his grandmother put together. And that was really saying something.

Spencer depressed the gas pedal. He was going to take Brenna home and make wild, passionate love to her until they both collapsed. Then he'd make slow, sweet love to her until that sharp tongue of hers was too tired to throw any more barbs his way. Then maybe he'd make love to her one more time—

Her voice sliced through his musings. "Maybe we should go back." There was a distinctly uneasy edge to her words. "We left the cabin unlocked and the siphon running."

The last thing on his mind was the unlocked cabin, but she did have a point. One his grandmother was no doubt going to make with much displeasure after the local police called her.

"Uh, I don't think going back is a good idea at the moment. I'm sure the officer will secure the scene."

"Uh-huh. Well, then, I think that siren is for you."

Spencer jerked his gaze to the rearview mirror. A police car barreled up behind them.

"Are you going to tell the nice officer I was kidnapped, or shall I?"

7

SPENCER SLUMPED in relief as the police car, siren blaring, tore past them up the road.

"For a minute there I thought we were in trouble," he said.

"*You* are."

He gave her a penetrating look before turning his attention back to traffic. A few seconds later, he pulled off the highway.

"This isn't my exit," she pointed out.

"I know. I need to swing by my apartment."

"I don't want to go to your apartment. I want you to take me home."

"My place is closer and I live alone. If we go to your house, your grandfather is going to get upset."

"But I need a change of clothing. I'm a mess."

His lips twitched. "I did notice. Relax. You can take a shower at my place. I promise."

"Really? And what am I supposed to put on afterward? Or do you keep a supply of women's clothing on hand at your place too?"

His grin could melt stone. "I probably have something you can borrow."

"I'd rather go home."

"And how are you going to explain to your grandfather why you look like you've been running through the forest?"

She looked down at her shoes with the drying mud clinging to them and brushed futilely at a grass stain on her pant leg. "I'll simply tell him the truth. It's all your fault." The darn man had the nerve to smile.

"Just tell me he isn't a gun collector."

"No," she said with mock sweetness, "but Uncle Bart is. I'm sure he'll lend Grandpa something appropriate."

His lips edged upward again. "Are you ever at a loss for words?"

Yes. Every time he touched her. All her logic short-circuited and she lost the power of speech, common sense and resistance. And when he wasn't touching her, her body was remembering and craving more.

He turned into the parking lot of a low, white brick complex. "See, I told you my place was closer." Instead of killing the engine, he twisted to look at her. "If you really want to go home, I'll take you. I just thought we should talk in private."

Puppy-dog eyes. The darn man had puppy-dog eyes. Soft, caramel brown. She lowered her gaze to her lap to avoid looking at him. Looking at him only got her into trouble.

Sighing, Brenna turned her head away, and eyed the garden apartments. "Okay, let's go in, but you'd better have plenty of hot water and coffee. You have a lot of questions to answer."

"Fair enough. While you shower, I'll put the coffee on."

As they walked to his front door, Spencer tried to remember the current state of his apartment. Uh-oh. Brenna would think he was a slob. While the apartment probably didn't qualify as a pigsty, he wasn't going to win any housekeeping awards.

"Uh, look, I'm afraid it's going to be a bit messy," he said, reaching for the key and wishing he'd taken time to pick up yesterday like he'd intended.

"Oh?"

He opened the door and groaned. There were socks on the floor. An untidy stack of magazines and soda cans sat on an end table. An open bag of popcorn lay overturned on the couch. The dining-room table held a briefcase and a spill of papers.

And the box.

Everything else receded in importance. Brenna would flip if she got a look at his sisters' box of gag gifts for the wedding shower. She'd be convinced he was a pervert. Maybe he could hide them in the spare bedroom closet before she saw the contents. Had the girls left anything else around he should be worrying about?

His entire family liked to tease him about his extensive social life and they weren't above playing a prank or two. Being the youngest could be a real pain at times.

He saw Brenna note the jacket tossed on the back of a chair and the empty microwave dinner carton sitting next to a glass that had once held something white— probably milk. Spencer cringed.

"The maid quit," he said desperately.

"I don't blame her."

"Hey, it's not that bad." He scooped up the pile of newspapers from the chair by the door. "It's just a little messy."

"Uh-huh. I can't wait to see the bathroom."

Oh-oh. How bad was the bathroom? Wasn't there a pair of briefs lying on the floor?

"Umm…let me go in first."

"Good idea. Better go armed. No telling what might be living beneath the rubble."

"Very funny."

She looked down at her shoes. "You want to give me one of those newspapers? I don't want to add mud to the rest of the mess."

He handed her the comic section from last week's Sunday edition and hurried to snatch up the box. Talk about making a lousy impression. He set the box on the floor of the spare closet, grateful that at least this room wasn't too bad. The daybed was made and the desk with all his computer equipment just looked cluttered. He hoped she wouldn't look under furniture. He was pretty sure he was raising entire colonies of dust bunnies since the last time he'd done a thorough cleaning.

At least the bathroom wasn't horrible. Even the toilet seat was modestly lowered. *Some* lessons stayed with a man who had older sisters.

He snatched up a wadded towel and washcloth and the pair of navy briefs, stuffed the shaving cream and toothpaste inside the open vanity and ran the towel over the inside of the basin to remove a few stray hairs. When he turned, Brenna stood in the doorway watching him.

"See? The health department would only give me a warning."

"Uh-huh."

She stared at the briefs dangling from his hand beneath the other clothing he'd collected along the way. Spencer tried not to blush as he stepped past her and opened his bedroom door.

Oh no, the red satin sheets his brothers had given him as a joke were on the unmade bed. Spencer tossed the dirty clothes in the general direction of the bed and shut the door.

"I'll get you some fresh towels," he offered quickly, wondering if she'd glimpsed the mess inside his bedroom. The floor was a land mine of ratty shoes.

"What am I going to change into?" she asked.

"Let me check the closet in the spare room and see if I have anything belonging to one of my sisters."

"How many do you have?"

He grimaced. "Unfortunately, two. Both older."

"So you're the baby?"

"They like to think so."

Spencer opened the closet, took one look at the sheer negligee hanging there and pulled the door shut. If Brenna saw that, he was a dead man.

"I'll check my room."

As he stepped past her, Brenna reached out and re-opened the closet door. Boldly draped over the diaphanous gown was a feather boa. He would strangle his sisters next time he saw them. They could at least have warned him about the nightgown.

"Your sisters wear this when they come to visit?" Brenna's gaze dropped. Too late, he realized the box holding the sex toys was gaping wide open.

Spencer made a grab for her shoulder, but Brenna was already bending over, lifting the top item. "Padded handcuffs? Velvet whips? Life-size...oh."

Her stunned gaze went to his ruddy face.

His eyes closed and he took a step back.

"You want to explain?" she asked.

His mouth opened and closed. Words failed him. No matter what he said at this point, she was bound to believe the worst. He opened his eyes.

"No," he finally managed.

"No?" Incredulous, she stared at him.

He shook his head sadly. "I don't think so."

"Try."

"Okay. Would you believe all that stuff belongs to my sisters?" He waited, holding his breath.

"No."

"Didn't think so." He turned and left the bedroom.

"Where are you going? You can't not explain!"

Stunned, Brenna followed him into the master bedroom, noting the beautiful brass headboard and the large, wide bed. She shied away from that, examining the rest of the room.

Neatness definitely wasn't one of his character traits. Small piles of clothing littered the dresser. Shoes were sprinkled across the carpeting. A weight set took up most of one corner along with a treadmill and small television. The room was messy and crowded, but not really dirty. There weren't even any crumbs on the red satin sheets.

"Red satin sheets?"

Spencer didn't answer. His embarrassment was almost tangible. He opened his closet and a basketball bounced out. Brenna sidestepped and watched him riffle through clothing before he finally pulled out a pair of white leggings.

"I thought I remembered seeing these in here the other day."

"They look a little small. Don't you have trouble getting them on?"

"Funny." But he wouldn't meet her eyes.

"What does your family do, leave a trail of clothing behind everywhere they go, like breadcrumbs?"

Spencer made a face as he pulled out a Redskins T-shirt and handed it to her along with the leggings. "Here. I'll throw your dirty stuff in the washer."

"Do you know how long denim takes to dry?"

"Do you want a shower or not?"

"Yes, please."

"Here. Clean towels," he offered.

She took the set of blue towels and decided to let him off the hook. He was so obviously embarrassed, she felt almost guilty. After all, her own apartment in New York wouldn't stand an inspection at the moment either. She'd packed in a hurry before coming here this weekend.

"Thanks. I won't be long."

"There's shampoo and soap in the bathroom. If you need anything else, just yell. I'll go put on the coffee."

It was awfully hard not to like him. But what was he doing with a closetful of sex toys and red satin sheets? Silly question. She knew exactly what he was doing and the knowledge bothered the heck out of her.

Not because she was a prude, she assured herself. Nor because she was jealous. After all, Spencer was a grown man. Yes, indeed. And he could do whatever he wanted with another consenting adult. She just wished it wasn't so easy to envision what he liked to do.

She turned her attention to the shower. Getting clean again felt wonderful. When she finally stepped from the tub she saw her pile of dirty clothing had disappeared. She hadn't even heard him come in.

Probably just as well. His sheets and his toys were giving her enough wild ideas after the intimate moments they'd shared. Ideas she shouldn't be entertaining. Twice now, she'd come within seconds of making love with this man. It would never do. He was a stranger. Even if he wasn't a thief, she had a life and a career waiting for her. She'd be going home on Sunday. Nothing permanent could come of a liaison with Spencer Griffen.

The leggings were small, but since he'd taken her panties along with everything else, she had no options. His T-shirt hung to mid thigh making the outfit close to decent. She used his comb on her wet hair, but found no sign of a hair dryer.

Stepping into the hall, she was rewarded by the scent of coffee. "Spencer? Do you have a hair dryer?"

He appeared at the other end, a wire whisk in his hand. "No. Sorry."

"That's okay. I'll just leave it wrapped in a towel. I want some of that coffee. Your whisk is about to drip."

He appeared momentarily at a loss, then looked down and cupped the whisk with his other hand, disappearing in the direction of the kitchen.

"What are you making?"

"Banana nut muffins."

"You can cook?"

"Anyone who can read can cook. You just follow the directions on the mix."

"I'm impressed. Most guys don't bother."

"Most guys don't have two sisters and a mother who believe all males should be house-trained. My two older brothers got the same lessons I did."

"Oooh. I like your family. Even if you do need a refresher course."

"Yeah. You'd fit right in." The thought didn't seem to make him happy. "Cream and sugar?"

"Black's fine." She watched him pour batter into greased muffin tins and put them in the oven.

"Look, would you mind if I take a quick shower while the muffins bake?"

Mind? Of course she'd mind. She could already picture him naked again. "Go right ahead."

"Thanks. Make yourself at home. I'll be right back."

Brenna sipped thoughtfully at her coffee, deciding to take him at his word. He'd been busy while she'd been in the shower. Most of the clutter had disappeared, confirming her earlier opinion that the apartment was simply messy, not really dirty. She bent and retrieved a slip of paper that had fallen to one side of the waste basket.

The lipstick smear in place of a signature caught her attention. Who was Valentino? A sister would hardly sign a message with a kiss. He'd lied to her. She crumpled the message and tossed it in the wastebasket.

Another message on strongly scented lavender paper was tacked to his refrigerator. Brenna set aside her qualms and scanned the feminine text.

> Hey, sexy, don't forget to bring the wine. I'll provide everything else. Eleven o'clock sharp. XXOOXXOO
>
> Alison

A disquieting tension gripped her stomach. Brenna found herself peering around more closely. Her gaze settled on a calendar hanging near the telephone. The bevy of models in their sexy poses and skimpy bikinis made her lips purse in annoyance.

The man certainly had a full life. His calendar was crammed with names and times, but it was the number of female names that grabbed her attention. Alison and Sylvia's names occurred frequently. There were also several dates listing Marilyn and Jayne, in addition to Liz, Jill, Betty and Jolie. He even had multiple names on a single day.

"Talk about stamina," she muttered. No wonder he was so good at seduction. The man kept a veritable harem. How did he keep them all straight?

Brenna tried to curb her rising annoyance. What difference did it make if Spencer saw a different woman every night? His sex life was none of her business.

Her nails drummed the countertop.

So the sex toys belonged to his sisters, huh?

Brenna heard the shower start. Before she realized her intention, she found herself heading for the spare bedroom.

Okay, so she was perverse, but she really wanted another look at the contents of that box. She'd never seen anything like those items up close before.

The handcuffs fascinated her. She could just picture some sexy woman stretched out on his red satin sheets wearing the fluffy lingerie from the closet. The woman would be handcuffed to his headboard, waiting for him to pleasure her.

And as Brenna already knew, he'd do a terrific job of that. No man had ever aroused her as quickly and completely as Spencer Griffen had. She eyed the realistic vibrator and felt a ripple of perverse excitement.

"Get a grip here," she muttered, mentally putting Spencer in those brief little briefs he'd taken from the bathroom earlier. Just how many women had helped him peel those briefs down his muscular thighs?

The telephone rang and Brenna jumped. It trilled again and Brenna heard the shower stop. She rushed across the room and picked up the receiver knocking several diskettes to the floor.

"Hello?"

"Is Spencer there?"

The sexy, throaty voice went perfectly with Brenna's image of some femme fatale wearing that scandalous nightgown. Brenna pictured a six-foot model with lipstick to match the sheets and a cigarette dangling between perfectly manicured fingers. She hated the woman, sight unseen.

Brenna pitched her own voice a bit lower in an effort to sound sultry. "He is, but I'm afraid he can't come to the telephone right now." The words sounded like she was staking a claim. Well, he deserved it after all he'd put her through. "I'm afraid *he's* still in the shower," she purred.

"Oh." Sexy Voice seemed surprised. "May I leave a message please?" she asked.

"I suppose, but he's going to be *very* busy for a while." Brenna felt decidedly wicked and immediately contrite. What was she doing? Spencer would kill her.

"I see." The voice almost sounded amused. "I'm

sorry to have...disturbed the two of you. This is Regina Griffen. Would you ask him to give me a call...when he gets free?"

Regina...oh, no. "His grandmother?" Brenna bit her tongue too late to stop her squeak of surprise. A low chuckle sounded in her ear.

"Yes. You really don't need to defend your territory quite so strenuously. I promise to keep my conversation with him short."

"Oh. Mrs. Griffen, I'm so embarrassed."

Mortified didn't come close. She'd told his grandmother he was in the shower. She'd implied she'd been in there with him.

"Not at all, my dear. Hygiene is very important."

"Oh, God." Brenna closed her eyes and prayed for an earthquake.

"Are you still there, dear?"

"I'm afraid so. There's never a convenient earthquake when you need one."

Regina Linnington Griffen laughed out loud. For a woman who had to be in her seventies, she had a sexy laugh. But then, Brenna probably just had sex on the brain.

"I don't think the Washington, D.C. area is prone to them, dear."

"Of course not," she agreed morosely.

Amusement continued to lace his grandmother's words. "Have you known Spencer long?"

"Long enough to want to throttle him."

"That long, hmm?" The throaty chuckle came again.

"Mrs. Griffen, the shower just stopped. Would you like me to go get him for you? I don't mean I'd go in there and get him, I mean I'd knock on the door and..." Brenna stared at the handcuffs still in her hand

and knew she was blushing even brighter than Spencer had when he opened the closet.

"That's quite all right. There's no hurry. Just ask him to give me a call when he has a moment."

"Yes. Of course."

"It was delightful talking with you. I do hope we'll get a chance to meet. No one has treated me as a threat to the male of the species in many years. I find it a tremendous boon to an aging ego."

Brenna had no idea how to reply to that, so she didn't. She managed to say goodbye before replacing the receiver. When she looked up, Spencer stood in the doorway staring at the handcuffs clutched in her fingers.

He wasn't wearing a shirt and his well-muscled chest was spotted with water that coursed across the flat planes of his stomach to disappear beneath his unsnapped jeans. Brenna couldn't tear her eyes from the sight.

"You surprise me," he said, running a towel briskly over his wet hair and down his chest. "I didn't think you were that sort of woman."

Spencer knew when she finally registered the meaning behind his words. She gripped the handcuffs more tightly and turned a brilliant shade of dusky rose, reminding him of his niece when he caught her with her hand in a bag of chocolate chip cookies.

"I have ruled out ant hills and throttling," Brenna enunciated slowly.

"Ant hills?" he questioned, but Brenna was on a tear again.

She nodded. "Fire ants," she said with emphasis as if that explained everything. "And only luck has kept me from coming up with a suitable replacement form of torture. But I will. And when I do, Spencer Griffen, you are going to suffer."

He wanted to laugh out loud. Instead, he deliberately stared at the handcuffs. "I think I'm going to look forward to that."

"Oh, no. No, you don't. I'm not kidding." She strode across the room to stand in front of him, waving the ridiculous handcuffs. "Do you know who that was on the telephone?"

"Nope. That's what I was going to ask you."

"Your grandmother was on that phone! I just made a complete idiot of myself. And it's all your fault!"

"My grandmother?" Fear replaced his humor. "What did she say?" He gripped her forearm. Brenna's expression immediately changed.

"It's okay, Spencer. She didn't sound upset or anything. She wants you to call her."

"Damn." He was going to have to tell her he didn't have the painting.

The timer on the stove buzzed loudly. Spencer snatched at the reprieve. He didn't want Brenna to overhear his conversation with his grandmother. He released her arm and tried to smile.

"Look, would you go pull the muffins out? I'd better call her back right away."

"But—okay."

"I'll be right out."

Brenna exited the room, still holding the handcuffs.

Spencer picked up the receiver and dialed the familiar number. Despite his worry, he smiled inwardly. He doubted Brenna realized she was still carrying the handcuffs with her. Maybe he could talk her into giving them a try before he had to return them to his sister. Now that he thought about it, there could be a lot of fun in a pair of handcuffs.

"Spencer, I didn't expect you to call me right back," his grandmother said when she answered. "I just wanted to invite you to a small dinner party tomorrow night."

"I didn't get the painting," he told her.

"I know, dear. You would have called."

"I'm going to try again tonight."

"No! Spencer, this has gone far enough. I will not have you put at risk over this."

"What about the risk to you and the campaign?"

"I have survived much worse in my seventy-six years. I am certain I can weather this storm as well."

"And the campaign? Will it survive once the media finds out?" He gripped the receiver hard.

"I certainly hope so. I'd like to think all the things your grandfather and I have done to fight child abuse are more important than one little act of youthful rebellion fifty years ago. Now forget about the painting and tell me you'll be here for the dinner party. Senator Shultz is planning to attend. It's important we impress him."

"You always impress people."

"Thank you, dear. Oh, and Spencer, do feel free to bring the lovely young lady who answered the telephone. We had a delightful chat."

"Is that why she was redder than those sheets Clark and Errol gave me for my birthday?"

His grandmother chuckled. "Did she like them?"

"You are a dirty old lady."

"Thank you, dear. Will I see you tomorrow?"

"Of course."

"Seven-thirty. See you then."

"Yes, ma'am."

He headed to the kitchen and found Brenna placing sectioned grapefruit halves on the table. She'd already set the muffins in the center on a plate. The handcuffs made a bizarre centerpiece.

"Everything okay?" she asked.

"Fine. My grandmother wanted to invite us to dinner tomorrow night."

"Us? What us? There is no us."

"There is now. My grandmother thinks you're delightful. I'm certain she's already picking out the caterer."

"What caterer? What are you talking about?"

"For the wedding." He poured fresh coffee into both their mugs, enjoying her confusion. "Our wedding."

"Spencer, if you're trying to get me to forget all the things I want to say to you—"

"I'm serious." He picked up a muffin and tore it in half. Steam rose, bringing the sweet scent of bananas to his nose. There was something a little scary about the domesticity of this scene, but he ignored the sensation. "What did you say to her?"

"Nothing!" But Brenna wouldn't meet his eyes. "I just told her you were in the shower."

She probably had. Knowing his grandmother, she'd taken it from there. The women in his family had been earnestly trying to marry him off for the past couple of years.

"Okay," he told her. "Forget it. Let's start with what you were doing in Hadden's bedroom."

"What about what you were doing there?"

"Never mind about me."

She picked up a knife and reached for the margarine. "Oh, but I do mind. I mind very much."

Spencer found himself riveted by the action of her knife gliding over the roll. There was nothing sexual, yet he couldn't tear his eyes away.

"Does your grandmother know what you do for a living?" Brenna asked.

"Of course."

She stopped buttering her muffin, raised the knife and stared at him. "And she approves?"

"She likes to boast about my career. I was valedictorian of my graduating class."

"You're making that up."

"Nope. Gospel truth. I can still remember most of the speech I had to give. Want to hear it?" He took the tub from her, slathered margarine on his own muffin and took a big bite, satisfied that he'd thrown her a curve and shaken off the strange spell she'd cast.

Brenna set down the knife and lifted her spoon. She dipped into the grapefruit and smiled up at him. "I guess that depends on who you stole the speech from. Was it anyone famous?"

He nearly choked on the bite of muffin. She batted her sooty black eyelashes at him and demurely began to chew the slice of grapefruit.

The chuckle built deep in his belly, exiting as a fullthroated laugh. Spencer picked up his napkin, wrapped it around the tines of the fork and began to wave it in the air.

"I surrender. You win."

A smile lit her face. "Good. Are you really a thief?"

He dropped the fork and sighed. "You mean professionally?"

"There's another kind?" She arched one eyebrow.

He'd always wanted to be able to do that. It frustrated him that she could do it and he couldn't.

"Hadden Senior has something that belongs to me," he told her. "I was trying to get it back."

"Why didn't you simply ask H.T.?"

"H.T.?"

"That's what we call Hadden when we're trying to tease him."

"You know him well enough to tease him?"

"I've known him since I was a kid. He's engaged to one of my best friends."

"The redhead. The real Kerry Martin."

"Yes."

"So what *were* you doing under the bed?"

Brenna set down her spoon. "The same thing you were doing.   I was there to get the painting."

His heart started pounding. "What do you know about the painting?"

"I know I have to find it before the appraisers do."

"Are we talking about the same painting?"

"I don't know. How many nudes did your grandmother pose for?"

She knew about the painting. How the hell could she know? "Who else knows?" he asked hoarsely.

"Hopefully, no one."

He scowled at her. "What do you want with it?"

"None of your business."

"The hell it isn't. It's exactly my business. The painting belongs to my grandmother."

"It does not! Hadden promised to give it to my grandfather. They were supposed to meet for lunch the week after he died."

"Your grandfather? What the hell does he have to do with anything?"

"Well, who do you think painted the picture?"

"Your grandfather?"

"Of course, my grandfather. Who did you think I was?"

"The most aggravating, maddening, sexy woman I've ever met!"

8

"YOU THINK I'M SEXY?" Brenna picked up her knife again and began spreading margarine with long slow strokes.

Spencer tore his attention from the mesmerizing action. "I'm trying not to think about you at all," he said defensively. "You've screwed up everything since I found you hiding under the bed."

That got her full attention. She stopped making him crazy with the knife and glared at him.

"*I've* screwed up? If you hadn't come in that night and been so darn noisy, I could have searched the place and been out of there with no one the wiser. Then we wouldn't be hiding from the police."

Guilt assailed him. "Brenna, about the police…"

A contemplative expression crossed her face. "We aren't really hiding from the police, are we?"

Uh-oh. How had she made that deductive leap so fast?

"And that wasn't really a police car coming up my street last night, was it?"

Spencer toyed with his spoon. "I didn't get a clear look," he temporized.

"And you aren't really a thief at all, are you?"

"Well, not by profession," he admitted.

She waved the knife at him. "So what was that all about last night and this morning?"

"Uh, Brenna, you want to put that knife down?"

"Yes. It isn't sharp enough for what I have in mind."

"Look," Spencer placated, "I think we've been at cross purposes all along. We're both after the painting. If Hadden is such a friend of yours, just ask him to give it to you and we can all relax."

She scowled. "I did ask. He said I could have it—" she dropped the knife with a clatter "—after the appraisers were done."

"Hell."

"Exactly."

Spencer pushed back his chair. "We have to get that painting."

Brenna nodded and bit into a wedge of muffin, momentarily diverting his attention as he watched her dab at a crumb with the tip of her tongue.

He told himself there was nothing erotic in her actions. He told himself to simply ignore her.

Yeah, right. He hadn't been able to ignore her from the moment they met.

Spencer eyed the handcuffs. He was having some interesting, if kinky thoughts about those handcuffs—and Brenna.

"We'll just have to go back inside tonight," she said thoughtfully.

That stopped his wayward thoughts. "Whoa, wait a minute. *You* aren't going anywhere. I'll go back to the estate this afternoon."

"Oh, really?" She raised a single eyebrow again. "Don't you think it will be a bit crowded?"

"What are you talking about?"

"Hadden's house is being used for a special FONZ meeting this afternoon."

"The character from that television show?" he asked skeptically.

"Friends of the National Zoo," she corrected.

"Why are they meeting at the estate? They have an entire zoo to meet at. Never mind. I'll just get in by pretending to be one of the members."

Brenna shook her head and the towel slipped over one eye. Frustrated, she freed her wet hair and let it fall in damp tangles around her face.

"It won't work, Spencer. This isn't a party where you can walk in and mingle. Why take chances? Better if we go in tonight."

"There is no *we* about it. I'm going in alone."

"Want to bet?"

Spencer tried to focus his aggravation, but he was distracted when she lifted her cup and took a small sip. Damn it, what fascinated him about her? She wasn't strikingly beautiful. Her eyes were too wide, her lips too full... Yet, as he watched her swallow, he thought of all the wonderful things she could do with those soft full lips and he had to restrain a groan.

This attraction was dangerous. Brenna wasn't the sort of woman he could have a fun fling with. She was the sort who would tie a man in knots until he stood at the other end of a church aisle watching her approach in a long white dress.

No. Oh, no. He had no plans to take that step with anyone right now. He was on the fast track to making partner. His top priority was work. Marriage and children had to wait. Women were a serious distraction. That's why he played the field.

Brenna was already more of a distraction than most, and he hadn't even gone to bed with her.

Yet.

He grew hard as he watched her nibble on another bite of muffin. It was so easy to imagine what it would feel like to have those teeth nibbling on him instead.

Brenna was startled when Spencer suddenly stood and began to pace. He looked like a man in pain.

"Don't worry," she hurried to assure him. "I won't get in your way. It will be faster with two of us. Hadden and Kerry are going to her parents' house for dinner tonight and then on to a party his cousin is having."

Spencer stopped pacing to loom over her. She tried to move her gaze upward, but found it focused on the tight denim of his slacks instead. She could clearly see the outline of his hard shaft pressed against the material. Her mouth went dry while her insidious body dampened in anticipation.

"How do you know all these things?" he demanded.

Brenna jerked her eyes away. She ran her fingers through her damp hair, hoping it didn't look as wild and uncontrolled as she felt.

"I've pumped Kerry for so much information, she probably thinks I'm interviewing for a job as her social secretary." Spencer's gaze focused on her chest. Brenna looked down. Her nipples were clearly visible, pressed against the thin fabric of the T-shirt.

"You know," she told him, suddenly nervous, "I should put my wet jeans in your little dryer over there."

Spencer lifted his gaze to hers. "I'll do it."

"No." Hastily, Brenna pushed back her chair and stood. "It's okay, I'll take care of it."

They faced each other only feet apart. Her heart started pounding like it did every time he touched her. She had to get control here. Just because she was dangerously attracted to him was no reason to act like some sex-starved female looking for a quickie.

Spencer suddenly smiled, a wolfish, masculine smile that reminded her of a predator sensing prey.

Brenna *felt* like prey, mesmerized, unable to look away. His kisses rocked her foundations and he only had to touch her to rouse every spark of feminine desire within her. It was frightening what this man did to her senses, but useless to pretend any different. She wanted Spencer on some elemental level she didn't understand.

"Am I making you nervous, Brenna?"

"Yes."

"Come here."

The softly spoken command started an inner tremor that weakened her knees. She wanted to do what he asked.

"My jeans," she managed to protest.

"Later."

Something rough and enticingly masculine entered his tone. His steady gaze never wavered. Ribbons of yearning fluttered against her insides. No man had ever looked at her quite like that, or made her feel so desirable.

"Come here," he repeated.

A ridiculous quiver of passion ran the length of her. She managed to shake her head, but he only continued to watch her from eyes that saw past her normal barriers to the woman beneath who wanted nothing more than to yield.

"Kiss me," he pressed in subtle demand.

All the oxygen flowed from her mind, making her dizzy. Brenna tried to remember all the reasons kissing him was a bad idea. She'd almost come up with one by the time she crossed the few feet separating them.

"I shouldn't," she told him, stopping close enough to smell the spicy scent of his aftershave.

"No," he agreed.

She edged closer. Her breasts tightened in unbearable anticipation. She wanted him.

"You short circuit my brain," she told him.

Mesmerized by the hunger in his potent look, she trembled as he slowly trailed a sizzling path down her cheek with his hand. Her body yearned for a release only he could bring.

"You make me crazy," he agreed softly.

Her nipples throbbed. The seam of the too-tight leggings pressed against her intimately, making her want to squirm against the sensation and the growing dampness she could feel there. No one had ever made her feel this breathless expectation. Spencer was seducing her with just a look. And she wanted to be seduced, even if he was all wrong for her.

"Are you going to kiss me?" she asked.

"Of course not."

Why did she feel a pang of loss at his answer? "It would be foolish."

"Yes," he agreed, leaning forward.

Their lips met in a delicate kiss. Her heart stopped, then plunged into a rhythm so powerful Brenna was afraid it would tear through her chest.

She leaned against him, surrendering to the touch of his hand where it flattened against the middle of her back. His other hand guided her head so his lips could cover hers in insistent passion. Heaven.

Brenna wriggled closer still, electrified by the probing of his tongue. His scent intoxicated her. She stroked the hard ridges of muscle that rippled across his back. So strong. So male.

When he insinuated his hand between their bodies, sliding it beneath her shirt, the astonishing touch of his blunt fingers on her exposed breast left her gasping.

Suddenly, it didn't matter that he was all wrong, that nothing permanent could come from this. Brenna was frantic to touch and be touched. She tugged at his shirt. A loose button tore free in her haste, momentarily stopping the incredible pleasure.

"Easy," he whispered, half laughing.

"But, you don't have any buttons to undo on me," she complained.

He chuckled, a throaty masculine sound that sent shivers down her spine.

"Good point, and I do have more shirts. Okay, tear away. I like seeing you this way."

"What way?"

He kissed her again, long and hard, drawing the soul from her body. This was how a kiss should be. He dropped his hand to cup her buttocks and pulled her more firmly against his thighs.

"You're all hot and bothered," he said.

Her fingers somehow managed to free the last of his buttons. "Who's all hot and bothered?" Her lips tingled from his kiss. Her breasts ached from the friction of his body.

Spencer grinned. "I am."

"Good."

He groaned as her lips sought the skin of his chest. She licked at the tiny nub of his nipple, pinching it lightly between her teeth, satisfied when he made a low rumbling sound of pleasure.

"Wait," he pleaded.

He struggled to pull her T-shirt up and over her head. Brenna was just as frantic to remove the impediment his shirt presented. Hands tangled. Elbows bumped. They were laughing in breathless anticipation when her hair snarled around his watch. Gently, he freed her, nudging her backwards until she was up against the counter.

His hands spanned her waist, sliding beneath the waistband of her leggings. He edged them down until he could cup her bare buttocks, pulling her against his body.

"Oh!"

Brenna felt a rush of reckless, wanton abandonment as he traced a path between the clefts.

"Spencer!"

His lips covered hers, searing her with all manner of incredible sensations. And it wasn't enough! She reached for the snap on his jeans, but before she could do more than get it open, he rolled her pants down her legs until they bunched at her knees. Then he lifted her onto the cold hard surface of the countertop.

"Spencer! What are you doing?"

"Remember the painting of the woman by the waterfall? The woman on the rock ledge?"

Oh, yeah. She remembered. The woman lay on the rock with her legs spread wide enough to accommodate the man kneeling between them. One of her legs was draped over his shoulders. Another man stretched the woman's arms high above her head with one hand, teasing a hardened nipple with his other hand.

Brenna couldn't seem to breathe. Surely he wasn't suggesting... Her body tingled as Spencer rolled the leggings down and off, tossing them to the floor and baring her completely. He held her gaze. Then, he raised her arms over her head, holding her wrists captive in one hand while he continued to watch her.

"If I had some fresh fruit we could try that scene in the painting hanging near Hadden's desk."

"Spencer!"

His wicked husky laugh sent curls of desire licking through her. He sought her breast, sucking strongly. Brenna moaned at the wild, singing sensations. Her head pressed back against the hard wood of the cupboard while his mouth drove her crazy.

Just when she thought she couldn't stand any more, his head dipped lower, his tongue flicking at the skin across her belly. He released her hands.

"Part your legs," he whispered. "Just like the painting."

The erotic image was so strong, she shuddered. She should protest. Instead, she helped him place her legs on his shoulders, embarrassed and aroused at the same time. He scooted her forward until her buttocks barely rested on the counter—just like the woman sitting on the rock shelf in the painting.

"Spencer!"

"I'm going to taste you."

He traced a path of hot wet kisses across her abdomen, interspersing them with tiny licks of his tongue that made her shiver all over. She was alive with excitement and wild abandoned sensations.

He paused when he reached the spot where she most wanted him to be. His breath feathered across the curls of hair. "Do you want me to stop?"

"No!"

His smile was so hotly carnal she trembled, wanting him desperately. His fingers teased a nipple.

"But I need to touch you too," she protested.

"You will," he promised. "All over. This is just the appetizer." And his hand stroked her pubic hair before moving to cup the wetness below. And all the while, he watched her reaction.

No man had ever stared so intently while doing such brazen things to her body. The unnerving sensation only heightened her desire. She squirmed against his touch. He smiled that devil's smile.

"You're incredibly responsive," he said softly.

Slowly, he parted her with his finger, one blunt tip mingling with her dampness.

"So hot. You're wet for me. And tight," he added, slowly inserting the finger inside her.

Brenna tried to speak and couldn't. The commotion building inside her was unlike any she'd ever experienced. She clamped her thighs around his hand. "I can't take this."

His grin was pure sin. "Sure you can."

And he inserted a second finger, all the while watching her burn with need. His thumb nail flicked the sensitive nub, making her cry out.

"I want you, Spencer! Inside me."

"I am inside you. Can't you feel me?"

Brenna cried out, overwhelmed by the fantastic sensations.

"Spencer!"

"Do you like that?"

She couldn't answer. She could only grip his shoulders, straining against the powerful tumult taking her higher and higher. Abruptly, his mouth was where she needed it to be. The feelings were too strong, too needy. Her hips bucked, lifting her from the counter as her body strained against him.

He probed with his tongue, touching a spot that sent a cry from her lips. She clung to the back of his head as she convulsed against him.

Spencer finally lifted her away, gentling her with his hands and soft words of praise. Embarrassment filled her despite the exquisite pleasure he'd given her. She trembled all over as he held her against his body.

His arousal pressed against her thigh right through his jeans.

"Now let's try a scene from the painting in the garden," he suggested against her hair.

He rubbed his chest against her sensitized nipples. They tightened at the feel of his prickly chest hair. His erection jutted at the apex of her naked thigh.

"My turn," she whispered.

She could barely stand on her wobbly legs, so Spencer lowered Brenna onto a chair. He made no move to help her when she teased him by lowering the zipper, one slow inch at a time. He was afraid he'd come right there as she began placing fierce small kisses against the wall of his chest and the planes of his stomach.

His pants dropped to his ankles. He kicked free of them while her fingers toyed with the elastic band of his red briefs. He throbbed with need.

"Touch me," he growled, cupping either side of her head.

Like the beautiful siren that she was, Brenna smiled, a womanly smile of control. He knew he wouldn't last long under her ministrations. Watching her release had nearly sent him over the edge with her.

Brenna cupped him through the nylon. Spencer growled in satisfaction. She continued to smile in that sultry way as she released him from the tight confines of the nylon.

Her face came alive with an expression of heady delight. She stroked the rigid texture of his skin. Spencer nearly lost it then and there. Her fingers captured him. The combination of her expression and the feel of her hands on his skin was almost more than he could take.

She touched the drop of fluid that leaked from his tip and brought that finger to her mouth to taste it.

Spencer shut his eyes. "You're going to kill me," he told her.

"You invited me to touch."

"Touch. Not torture."

She stroked him lightly. "You call this torture?"

"When I want you this badly, it is. I'm in serious jeopardy of coming right here."

She blinked, apparently saw that he was serious, and her mouth closed over him.

"Brenna!"

His gasp fell somewhere between a plea and a moan. He was dangerously close to orgasm. Her lips were incredible, her mouth so hot that he finally pushed her away, unable to take any more. He drew her against his body, kissing her with fevered intensity.

"The bedroom," he whispered.

"The couch is closer."

"Yes."

He lifted her. She wrapped her legs around his waist as he carried her the few feet into the living room. The scent of their lovemaking clung to their damp bodies as he lowered her quickly, greedy to be inside her at last.

They were both shaking when he fitted himself against her, surging inside with one breathless stroke. She closed around him, a perfect sheath. He groaned in pleasure. Brenna smiled, tightening around him. He wanted to go slow, to savor the incredible excitement, but she began to move beneath him, lifting herself as if to absorb him completely.

His mouth closed over hers, swallowing her small sharp cries of pleasure as he withdrew and plunged into her again and again. She rose to meet each thrust, as if she'd never get enough of him.

"Brenna!"

Her release followed his, leaving them both spent and dazed by the intensity.

Spencer couldn't put a name to the strange feelings surging through him, but he knew he never wanted to let her go. As his heart rate steadied, he gently rolled off her to sit on the floor beside the couch. His hand stroked her belly, unwilling to sever the connection between them.

"You're incredible."

Spencer liked the light blush that added extra color to her cheeks.

"You were pretty good yourself."

He grinned at her saucy rejoinder and pressed a small kiss against the outside curve of her breast. "I do try."

Her expression shuttered instantly. What had he said? Was she feeling regrets? God, he hoped not. No one had ever made him feel so strong, so complete. He could go on touching her like this forever. The thought sent uneasy skitters racing through him.

He hadn't used protection.

He always used protection. The small foils were in his bedroom and in his wallet. There were probably some in the drawer on the end table right here in the living room. And he'd never once thought about using them.

"Damn. I didn't intend for this to happen."

Brenna sat up sharply. "Regrets already, Spencer?"

"Hell, no! But I didn't use protection."

The hostile look faded from her expression. "Oh."

"Oh? Is that an, oh, it doesn't matter, or an, oh, no, we're in big trouble?"

"I'm probably okay."

Spencer groaned. How could he have been so stupid? What if she got pregnant? The idea shouldn't hold this sudden sense of excitement. He should be feeling totally horrified at the possibility.

"I guess how big the trouble is depends on how healthy you are," she said.

"How healthy—?" His eyes narrowed. "I am perfectly healthy, Brenna. I always use protection."

She arched an eyebrow. "Really?"

"Until just now," he amended. "What about you?"

"You don't have to worry about me," she assured him.

Remembering how tight she'd been, how surprised she'd seemed by some of the things they'd done, he could well believe that. "Well, good."

"Yes. So now what?"

Spencer climbed to his feet. Brenna swung her legs off the couch.

He frowned. "How do you do that?"

"Do what?"

"Push all my buttons so easily? Do you realize you aggravate me with one breath while at the same time you turn me on without even trying?"

Her eyes widened. Her lips parted in surprise. "You can't be serious."

His passion was sated, but not this strange need for her. The dichotomy was making him increasingly uncomfortable.

"Don't look so panicky, I'm not Superman." But she made him feel like one. "I'll go put your jeans in the dryer."

He started toward the kitchen.

"Who's panicked?" she called out softly.

Spencer stopped in the doorway. He looked over his shoulder to find her watching, a provocative curve to her lips. Her bold gaze moved from his buns to his face—and she blew him a kiss.

Spencer knew he was grinning like a fool, but he didn't care. She was impulsive, daring, sexy and just plain fun. Her laughter followed him into the kitchen. If he'd made her pregnant, they were getting married and that was all there was to that.

He stepped into his briefs and picked up his jeans. He was in deep trouble here and he knew it. Far from working his desire for her out of his system, their phenomenal lovemaking had only left him craving more.

The knowledge scared him. So did the fact he hadn't even thought to take precautions. He'd never once forgotten before. But marriage to Brenna wouldn't be so bad. She was intelligent, attractive...she'd give him a beautiful child. Funny, until just this moment, he hadn't realized how much he did want children of his own...eventually.

"What did you mean when you said we both want the painting?" Brenna asked.

Her question pulled him from his strange musings and visions of a tiny baby nursing at her breast. Spencer whirled to find Brenna standing in the kitchen. She wore one of his long-sleeved flannel shirts, leaving her shapely legs tantalizingly bare.

"What?" He dragged his gaze from the sight to her kiss-swollen mouth.

"The painting belongs to my grandfather."

Her words cut through his distraction. "No way. It belongs to my grandmother."

Her lips firmed. "Let's get something straight right now, Spencer. The painting is mine when we find it."

"Not a chance. My grandmother is the subject."

"And my grandfather painted it."

"He sold it to Summerton."

She looked away, her expression guilty. "Both Hadden and *his* grandfather promised *my* grandfather he could have the painting back," she insisted.

"No."

Brenna planted her hands on her hips, molding the shirt to her body. "You can't tell me no. My grandfather *needs* that painting."

"For what?"

"I can't tell you." But she looked guilty again.

"Well, my grandmother needs it too."

"Why?"

"*Why?* Because she's the *subject*. You think she *wants* people to know she once posed in the nude?"

"What's the big deal? It isn't pornographic. It's art. Besides, she doesn't have to worry, my grandfather doesn't want to display the painting."

Spencer frowned. "Why not?"

"What do you mean, why not?"

"If he doesn't want to display it, why does he want to get it back so badly?"

Her lips set in mutinous lines. "He just does."

"Well, too bad. He isn't going to get his wish. The painting is going to my grandmother just as soon as we find the damn thing. And I'm not going to argue with you."

"Good, because the painting belongs to my grandfather."

"Like hell."

She held up a hand to stave off his protest. "Do you realize how pointless this discussion is since we don't even have the painting?"

"We'll get it. I'm going over there now."

"You'll be arrested."

How could he have thought she was fun? She was a pain in the neck. He just might throttle her after all. "Don't worry about me."

"I'm not," she huffed. "You can do whatever you please. Just have a friend standing by to post your bail. You do have friends, don't you?"

He really hated it when she used that syrupy-sweet tone of voice.

"I'll wait and get the painting this evening when the house is empty," she continued before he could respond. "After you've been caught."

"Why, you mouthy little brat, I don't plan to get caught."

"No one ever does."

Spencer took a step in her direction and stepped on something small and hard. He looked down to see the button from his shirt. The memory of how it got there disconcerted him for a second. "What made me think you were irresistible?"

Brenna glared right back. "I was wondering the same thing about you."

Someone rapped on his front door.

"Who's that?"

Spencer shook his head. "I don't know. I'm not expecting anyone. It's probably my neighbor looking to get up a game of basketball. Ignore it. He'll go away."

The knock came again, louder this time, more insistent.

"Maybe you'd better answer," she suggested nervously.

Spencer frowned. His frown turned to panic as they both clearly heard the key turning in the lock.

"Spencer?" a woman's voice called out. "Are you home?"

"Damn." He started forward knowing it was far too late. Marilyn was already inside.

"Oh, there you are. Don't tell me you just got out of bed, Valentino."

The teasing, deep contralto voice set Brenna's teeth on edge. So this was the woman who left lipsticked signed notes and a box full of sex toys in Spencer's apartment.

Brenna fought a wave of jealousy as she regarded the signs of their lovemaking sprinkled about the kitchen. She set her jaw, ignored the wadded T-shirt lying on the stove, stepped past the discarded stretch pants she'd been wearing, and headed for the doorway. She wanted a look at the sexy-voiced woman who called him Valentino.

"No, I didn't just get up," Spencer said in irritation, "and don't call me that."

He sounded embarrassed. Good. Brenna glanced down and unbuttoned her top button to display a little more cleavage. Satisfied, she stepped forward.

"What are you doing here?" Spencer was asking, sounding grumpy.

"It's Saturday, remember? And you won't believe what I found. That odd little shop had a game like pin-the-tail-on-the-donkey, only in this game you pin the appendage on...Oh, hello."

Brenna lounged back against the entrance to the kitchen and pasted what she hoped was a sultry smile on her face. His friend was extremely pretty...if surprisingly older than Spencer.

"Hello," Brenna responded.

"I didn't know you had company." The woman pushed back a strand of silky blond hair. "Am I intruding?"

"Not at the moment," Brenna assured her. "I'm Brenna."

Spencer closed his eyes.

"I'm Marilyn."

"It isn't what you think," Spencer said, opening his eyes.

"Really?" Marilyn tipped her head in obvious disbelief.

"I was talking to Brenna."

Brenna ignored him. Maybe she had no right, but Spencer had just made love to her. She was not going to stand here and pretend otherwise. If *Marilyn* didn't know she was one of a long list of conquests, Brenna would set her straight here and now. Brenna cringed at the thought that she was now one of them too. How many of his other women had keys to his apartment?

"Would you care for some coffee and a banana nut

muffin?'' Brenna offered sweetly. "Spencer just made breakfast."

"Brenna, Marilyn is my—"

"Thank you. If I wasn't running so late I'd take you up on that." Marilyn sounded amused. Her smile was open and friendly. "I didn't know Spencer could bake."

Darn. Brenna didn't want to like the woman. "Oh, you know Valentino," she said, "he's just full of surprises."

"Yes, isn't he? Have you known each other long?"

"Knock it off," Spencer warned.

Brenna wasn't sure who he meant, but Marilyn answered him. "Jayne is really going to be sorry she didn't come with me."

"Marilyn," he warned.

The blonde turned back to Brenna. "I hate to meet and run, but Spencer is right, I have to get my stuff and go. I guess you're in no condition to carry the box down to the car for me," she added in an aside to him.

"I'll carry the damn box," he snarled. "Just let me get my shoes."

"They're in the bedroom," Brenna said helpfully.

Spencer muttered something under his breath and started down the hall.

"Is there anything I can do to help?" Brenna asked.

Marilyn shook her head. "Spencer can handle one little box. If you'll excuse us for just a few minutes?"

"Certainly."

Spencer returned quickly. He'd stuffed his bare feet into running shoes, pulled on a clean navy polo shirt that emphasized his broad shoulders, and strode into the living room holding the box of sex toys and the sheer negligee from the closet. He thrust the latter into Marilyn's hand. "I'll be right back, Brenna. Listen, she's not—"

"Take your time," Brenna snapped. Valentino was in for a rude shock if he thought she'd stand around waiting for him to get rid of a former lover before he came back for her.

9

HADN'T SHE KNOWN the woman would be a blonde? Brenna fumed as she replaced the telephone. Her grandfather was probably on the golf course with his cronies. Brenna called for a taxi as she struggled back into the white leggings. She knocked as much mud as she could off her tennis shoes and headed downstairs.

Spencer stood next to a shiny red Lexus with his back to her. He was talking earnestly to Marilyn, who was also facing away from the door Brenna had just emerged from. The two of them peered at something on the back seat of her car. Brenna hoped he was having a terrible time explaining her presence in his apartment. Neither of them noticed as she walked quickly and quietly away and out of sight around the street corner.

How could she have been so stupid? He was single, sexy, and obviously well-to-do. Of course he had women. Probably dozens of them.

Including her.

Brenna cringed. She'd really played the fool falling into bed with him like that. Heck. They hadn't even made it to the bed! How could she have behaved so wantonly with a complete stranger? A stranger who was determined to get her grandfather's painting.

She couldn't let that happen. Whatever it took, she had to beat Spencer to the painting. Her grandfather was not going to jail if she could prevent it.

At the archway marking the entrance to the development, Brenna waited for the cab. Would Spencer be foolish enough to try and get inside the estate this afternoon?

What if he got to the painting first?

She'd steal it back.

The cab driver eyed her suspiciously when she flagged him down, but when she gave him her grandfather's address, he was willing enough to take her. He even waited patiently while she went inside for her purse and a generous tip. The telephone rang as soon as she returned upstairs.

Spencer's low rumble immediately filled her ear. "Brenna! Why did you leave like that?"

"Your apartment was getting a little crowded," she told him.

"That was my sister."

"Right. I've seen pictures of your sisters, remember? Neither of them is a sexy blonde."

"Marilyn dyed her hair."

"Before coming to pick up her sex toys?" Brenna inquired sweetly.

"Yes!"

"You're weird, Spencer."

"Listen to me. My sisters are throwing a surprise stag party for a good friend of theirs. That box of stuff is all intended as joke gifts and party favors."

"Your *sisters* are weird too."

"Brenna, both of them have children and they didn't want the kids finding that sort of stuff in their houses so they asked if they could store the box at my place until today. Honest. Just be glad you didn't see the cake in her car. I can't believe there's a store that makes anatomically correct cakes. It gives a whole new meaning to beefcake."

"Spencer—"

"Look, Brenna, I know I should have introduced

you, but frankly, Marilyn's unexpected arrival rattled me. Plus, she's a terrible tease and I was afraid of what she might say. Can we start over? Please?"

Could that woman really have been his sister instead of an ex-lover? Brenna tried to remember what his sisters looked like and failed. His sisters hadn't been the ones she'd been paying attention to in those pictures. And what difference did it make if the blonde was his sister or not? Brenna had no claims on Spencer Griffen.

"Brenna, we're losing sight of what's important here."

"My *grandfather's* painting?"

There was a moment of silence.

"Could we just agree that we have a day and a half to find that painting before the auditors arrive?" he asked.

She gripped the receiver more tightly.

"Now, rather than risk bumping into you in Hadden's bedroom, what do you say we combine forces?"

"I thought you wanted to go back to the estate alone."

"I changed my mind. Look, we'll get the painting and then worry about who it belongs to afterwards."

"We both *know* who it belongs to."

"Brenna."

Spencer was right. The most important thing was to get to the painting before the auditors did. With both of them searching, they could move through the house much faster.

"What did you have in mind?" she asked.

"How long is that FONZ meeting going to last?"

"I have no idea, but I'm telling you it will be safer to go in tonight when no one is home except the housekeeper and her husband. With any luck, they'll go out to a movie or something and we'll have the place to ourselves."

"And if they don't?" he asked.

"We'll have to be very quiet.

"I'll pick you up at six. We'll stop and grab something to eat on the way over there."

"Why?"

His exasperation was plain. "Because the food in jail is terrible. If we get caught, I don't want to rely on them to supply my dinner."

"That isn't funny, Spencer."

"You're telling me." His pause was longer this time. When he spoke again, his voice deepened. "Marilyn forgot the handcuffs," he said quietly.

A curl of unexpected excitement established itself in her lower abdomen. Brenna couldn't think of anything to say. Her imagination instantly created all sorts of scenarios involving those handcuffs and Spencer's big brass bed.

She cleared her throat. "I need to take a shower." What on earth had possessed her to say that?

"You just took one," he reminded her. "But I like picturing you there. Have you ever thought about standing under a shower while handcuffed to a soap dish?"

"What?!"

"I can see you there, Brenna, all pretty and wet while I lather your body with soap."

"Spencer!" Those shafts of excitement uncurled to go spinning around fast enough to make her light-headed.

"Want to come back over and give it a try? If you prefer, you can handcuff me to the soap dish."

The image excited her. "You're perverted," she whispered.

"That's your fault. I never had these kinds of fantasies until I started hanging around you. You make me think of all sorts of wild things I wouldn't mind trying."

Brenna's fingers were suddenly damp where they clutched the telephone. "You shouldn't have spent so much time looking at Hadden's erotica."

Spencer's husky laugh was a low sound that vibrated from her ear to her eager body. "That probably did give me a few ideas," he admitted. "Like the one we tried out on the kitchen sink."

"I don't want to talk about it."

"Me either, but I wouldn't mind a repetition. Did you see those sculptures in his bathroom?"

She had. "Women don't get turned on by that sort of thing." And she was lying through her teeth.

"You aren't just any woman, Brenna," he purred. "You liked what we did in the kitchen."

Darn him.

"And I saw the way you looked at some of those other paintings. Want to spend the afternoon trying a few of those poses?"

Yes.

"I'm hanging up now, Spencer." She had to hang up before her imagination took total control.

"Okay. I'll see you at six. And by the way, I'm very partial to black satin and lace."

Drat that man. Her lingerie drawer was full of black satin and lace.

"In your dreams, Griffen."

"Fantasies," he corrected softly before disconnecting.

Brenna stood holding the telephone, as agitated as a schoolgirl with her first crush.

SPENCER HAD TO CONTROL his impatience as he waited for six o'clock to roll around. Twice he almost went over to the Summerton estate by himself. But Brenna was right, it would be safer to go in again under cover of darkness. He'd taken a major risk two nights in a row and all he had to show for his efforts so far was Brenna.

"Not bad," he told himself. He checked the rearview mirror, changed lanes and moments later turned in to Brenna's neighborhood.

Brenna was skittish around him, but her jealous reaction to his sister and the passionate way she'd responded gave him hope. She intrigued him on so many levels he'd lost count. He wanted time to get to know her better.

Unfortunately, the painting that was drawing them together was also eventually going to pull them apart. He couldn't let anyone but his grandmother have that painting. There was no compromise here. This was too important.

Spencer pulled into her driveway and grabbed the light gray sports coat from the seat beside him. He'd dressed again in black, having to really hunt through his apartment to find his black mock turtleneck. The coat dressed up his casual attire, made it look more sophisticated instead of, well, like something a thief would wear.

Brenna answered the door before he could raise a hand to knock. "You're here," she greeted.

He found himself smiling at her breathy greeting. "And so are you."

She, too, was dressed in black. The one-piece jumper had a gold-threaded red belt that went with the red blazer she wore overtop. Take away the red and she'd be dressed as darkly as he was.

"Where else would I be?" she demanded.

"Well, I was sort of hoping for the shower."

She blushed, a pretty rosy pink.

"Brenna?" a new voice called out. "Is that your date?"

"Yes, Grandpa."

"Well, invite him in."

A panicked look crossed her face. Did she think he was going to blurt out something about the painting in front of her grandfather? Spencer stepped past her and into a gracious living room. A spry, rangy gentleman strode forward, sizing him up with shrewd gray eyes.

"Spencer Griffen," he said, stepping forward to take the strong hand in a firm clasp.

"B. J. Wolford," the other man said.

"B. J. Wolford?" Spencer shot Brenna a startled glance. She wouldn't meet his eyes. Wolford, not Lispkit. She'd lied to him! The little minx had lied to him again.

"You were expecting someone else?" His gaze went from one face to the other.

"Actually, sir, I think I was."

Brenna stiffened.

"Your granddaughter never mentioned your name when she spoke of you."

"Hmmph. My publicist would be appalled. Griffen, did you say?"

Spencer nodded.

"Any relation to Regina Linnington Griffen?"

"My grandmother."

His gaze flashed to Brenna. *"Really?"*

Brenna turned fire-engine red and stared at the thick white carpeting.

"It seems my granddaughter forgot to mention your name as well. How is your grandmother these days?"

There was something in the older man's voice when he mentioned Spencer's grandmother that made

Spencer suspect their relationship had gone beyond friendship.

"Quite well. You ought to give her a call. I'm sure she'd enjoy hearing from an old friend."

"Does she have a listed number?"

"No, but I'll be happy to give it to you." He recited the ten digits and wondered if his grandmother would thank him or skin him alive. On the other hand, his grandmother had caller-ID service. If she didn't want to take a call from B. J. Wolford, she wouldn't.

"Spencer, shouldn't we be leaving?" Brenna asked abruptly.

He debated making her sweat a little longer, but decided he wanted to ask his questions more. "Yes."

"Come back when we can sit and talk," her grandfather invited.

"I'd like that. And give my grandmother a call. I'm sure she'd enjoy hearing from you."

"I just may do that."

"Night, Grandpa." Brenna bussed his cheek and quickly took Spencer's arm, tugging slightly. "Don't wait up."

Her grandfather raised a single bushy eyebrow. He looked Spencer in the eye. "Don't let her talk you into anything reckless, son. My granddaughter can be a bit impulsive."

Spencer grinned. "I've noticed. Now that I've met you, I suspect she inherited that trait along with the ability to raise one eyebrow."

B. J. Wolford's seamed face split in a wide grin. "She did at that. Going to be the death of me yet, this girl."

"Don't worry, sir. I'll take care of her."

Her grandfather nodded seriously. "Yes, I can see that you will. Have fun."

Brenna whirled on Spencer as soon as they were outside. "What was that all about?"

"What?"

"That male-bonding scene between you and my grandfather."

"I like him."

"I like him too, but I am hardly a 'girl' and I don't need anyone taking care of me."

Spencer kept his smile tucked inside. "Brenna, if you think starting an argument with me is going to make me overlook the fact that you lied to me, forget it."

"I never lie!"

"Yeah? How come you let me believe your grandfather was Lispkit?"

Brenna stepped into his car and settled down staring straight ahead. "I never said he was Lispkit."

"Of course you did. You told me your grandfather painted the…" Spencer stopped. The odd little snippets of information began clicking into place. "Did your grandfather paint the nude?"

Brenna turned away.

"He did, didn't he? You didn't lie." He studied the back of her head. "If he's the real artist he must have signed Lispkit's name. I'm right, aren't I? And that's why you want the painting so bad."

Brenna turned to glare at him.

"But B. J. Wolford is famous. Why would he sign another man's name to one of his paintings?"

"Get in the car," she demanded.

Spencer shut the door and came around to the driver's side. He slid inside, buckled his seat belt and stared at her, waiting.

Brenna sighed. "He wasn't famous when he did the painting. Didn't your grandmother tell you about it?"

Spencer uttered a low, heartfelt curse. "No. She kept this little tidbit to herself."

"Probably to spare my grandfather. I think the two

of them were in love a long time ago. Anyhow, now you see why I have to get the painting back. Grandpa's reputation is at stake."

Spencer started the engine. "So is my grandmother's."

"It's hardly the same thing."

"She posed for the painting."

"So? My grandfather doesn't do erotica."

Spencer backed down the driveway and turned onto the street. "My grandmother was married to William Griffen."

He felt Brenna's startled gaze on him. "The Reverend William Griffen?"

"One and the same. Now *you* see the problem. Moral fiber? Family unit? Children are the backbone of the world? These phrases ringing any bells?"

"Your grandfather was famous."

Spencer nodded. "As his widow, so is my grandmother."

Brenna thought back to her brief telephone conversation with the woman and cringed.

"Look," Spencer continued, "the important thing here is to keep the painting away from outsiders. We can worry about what to do with the blasted thing once we get it out of the house."

"Agreed."

They had supper in a Chinese restaurant on the Rockville Pike, halfway between her grandfather's place and the Summerton estate. Amazingly, they had fun. They talked sports, movies and politics and didn't agree on anything except disaster movies and mystery novels.

"I still can't believe that was your sister," Brenna said suddenly.

"I promise. I'll give you a formal introduction. In fact, I'd take you over to the party, but they're going to play pin the missing parts on the cover model and I'm afraid that's just a little too much for my delicate sensibilities."

"Where did they find all that stuff?"

"Frankly, I was afraid to ask."

"Marilyn looked too young to be the mother of three kids."

"She's going to love you for that. Her youngest just started first grade. She lost thirty-seven pounds, dyed her hair blond and took up competitive running."

"You're kidding."

"Nope. Her poor husband is hard pressed to keep up with her. I'm glad she's his problem."

Brenna swatted him with her chopsticks. The waiter came over to ask if they wanted anything else and Spencer asked for the check.

"I've been thinking," he said more seriously. "Maybe you ought to call the estate and see if anyone is home."

Brenna sighed. Fun was over. For a while she'd managed to convince herself this was like a real date. Once they got the painting, would she ever see him again?

"What do I do if someone answers?"

"Ask if you left a sweater there or something. I figure if no one is home I can just park on the side street and we'll go in over the fence."

"Why do it the hard way? We can park two blocks over behind the estate and can go in through the back gate past the tennis court. The lock's broken. You seem to like climbing things, but I'd just as soon pass if you don't mind."

Spencer eyed her ruefully. "I suppose you have a key to get inside the house?"

She reached inside her jacket and produced a shiny bit of metal. "Kerry gave it to me the other day when she couldn't meet the florist. I never quite got around to giving it back. Beats the heck out of climbing trees."

He placed several bills inside the leather folder and reached for her hand. "You're something, you know that?"

"Of course. Wasn't there a telephone over by the door where we came in?"

THEY PARKED TWO BLOCKS away on a street behind the vast grounds of the estate. They took off their jackets, and Brenna led the way to the back gate. It was so well camouflaged that Spencer would have missed it completely if he'd been alone.

Brenna reached for the hidden latch and tugged. Her face, dimly revealed by the moonlight, had a startled expression.

"Something wrong?" he asked.

"It's locked."

"I thought you said the lock was broken."

"It was." She stared up at him. "I've got a bad feeling about this. If they fixed this lock, what else have they done?"

A chill that had nothing to do with the blowing wind crept right down his backbone.

"I'm sure they fixed the window you cut a hole in."

"And added alarms upstairs?" she asked.

"Possibly." He stared at the ten-foot fence. "Maybe we should reconsider."

"What choice do we have?"

She had a point. They had to get that painting.

"You want a boost up?"

Brenna stared at the gate. "I'd prefer an elevator. Gym was not my favorite class."

Spencer grinned and cupped his hands. "You prefer indoor sports, hmm?"

She stepped into his hands and he boosted her up.

162   *The Naked Truth*

God, the lady had a gorgeous backside. The thin material molded her cheeks for just a second as she began to climb.

"Keep your mind on the job, Griffen."

"I'm trying. God knows, I'm trying."

Brenna swung over the top. She started down the other side and disappeared behind a wall of greenery.

"You okay?" he called.

"Wonderful. Watch that last step."

Spencer followed her over.

They headed across the manicured grounds until they reached the path that twisted past the tennis court. A full-sized pool sat beyond that, dimly visible in the glow of the outdoor lighting. She started around the side of the house. Spencer grabbed her arm and tugged until she stopped. "There's an entrance right over there."

"This is the key to the front door."

"The doors have different locks?"

"I don't know. Do you want to take a chance?"

Spencer shook his head.

"Then be quiet and follow me."

Well, he'd known from the start she'd lead any man on a merry chase. But damn, she just might be worth the effort.

They came around the front of the house, skirting darkened windows with care. He pulled out his gloves and slipped them on. Brenna climbed the front steps as though she was an invited guest before he could stop her. She inserted the key and whipped out a white handkerchief as the wide oak door clicked open.

Spencer released a breath he hadn't even known he was holding. Brenna opened the door with the hand holding the handkerchief. They stepped inside the dark hallway and Brenna headed right for the security panel on the far wall. He watched her punch in a series of numbers.

"Oh, no!"

His heart slid into his throat. "What's the matter?"

"He changed the code."

A cold fist of fear slammed into his stomach. He rushed to her side.

"Try it again. Maybe you hit a wrong button."

"Spencer, we only have seconds!"

She was already rekeying the numbers. The light stubbornly remained red. Brenna looked up at him. The same fear somersaulting in his insides was mirrored in her expression.

"Run."

"What?"

"Run!" she repeated, and put her words into action. She whirled and sprinted for the front door. Spencer followed on her heels, pausing to shut and latch the door behind them just as all hell broke loose.

10

LIGHTS SUDDENLY BLAZED everywhere, highlighting the grounds around the house. An angry siren shattered the night.

Brenna fought abject terror and ran. Spencer pounded away beside her. Why had it never occurred to her that Hadden might change the security code?

They sprinted across the lawn and Spencer headed in a diagonal toward a line of dark evergreens. Brenna wanted to protest, but she needed her oxygen for running. Pine branches whipped against her body as they plunged into the thicket. His course had taken them beyond the reach of the lights that flooded the grounds.

Spencer reached the fence. "Climb," he ordered.

"But—"

"Later."

He boosted her up and Brenna began to climb. That's when she heard the dog.

"Oh, my God! When did Hadden get a dog?"

"Move!"

Brenna was up and over the fence, dropping into a thicket of juniper bushes in the neighboring yard. The scratchy, prickly plants clawed at her jumpsuit, irritating her skin wherever they made contact. Spencer landed next to her, grabbed her hand and took off running again.

Despite the raucous noise coming from the Summerton estate, no lights gleamed inside the neighbor's house which sat on a small rise in the center of the lot. From the noise at their backs, the dog had reached the spot where they'd gone over the fence. Spencer never glanced back, nor eased his killing pace.

They skirted a pool and found themselves in some sort of flower garden. Spencer discovered a gravel path and took it until he suddenly stopped with a curse.

"What?" she panted.

Spencer pointed. The back wall was just exactly that. A brick and concrete wall, at least ten feet high.

"How are we going to climb over that?"

His head moved slowly as he studied the situation. All Brenna could make out were shrubs and trees. He tugged her hand and she followed him to a tall crab apple tree. "We'll have to go up."

Brenna balked. "I'm not climbing that tree."

"You'd rather stay here and wait for the police? They should be along any second now."

The distant siren was audible, she realized. So was the barking dog. "Give me a boost?"

He cupped his hands and she reached for the lowest limb, scrambling awkwardly into the tree.

"How come you and I always end up in trees?" she panted.

"Must be you. I hate climbing trees." Spencer swung himself up beside her. "Keep climbing. The branches hang over the wall. No. Go to your right. Yeah, that's it."

Brenna felt the tree sway. Crab apples broke loose and scattered to the ground in a shower of dying leaves.

"Spencer, this branch doesn't feel very sturdy."

The branch began to wobble.

"Be careful," Spencer said. "Are you over the wall yet?"

Brenna looked down. A serious mistake. The ground lay far below, a dark, forbidding sight. She gripped the rough bark for all she was worth. "Almost."

"Keep going."

She heard an ominous creak. "Spencer, there's at least three feet between this branch and the top of that wall. What am I supposed to do?"

"Hold on and swing your leg over. You should be able to touch the top of the wall."

The man was crazy.

"Then what?"

"Then you'll have to straddle the wall and scoot forward until you reach the place where this wall butts to the Summerton fence. We can use the fence to climb down."

Completely crazy.

"No."

"You'd rather jump from the top of the wall?"

"I'd rather be home in bed," she muttered.

"Hell of a time to tell me that. Do you want me to go first?"

Brenna looked at the distance. She could not stand on that itty-bitty wall.

"Brenna, why don't you inch back and I'll go first?"

Brenna clung to the narrow branch and looked down at the top of the brick wall. The ground was a long way down. A very long way down. Fear gnawed at her.

"I can't."

The branch swayed ominously.

"Can't what?"

She heard another subtle, cracking sound. Brenna hugged the branch more tightly.

"I can't move."

"Why not?"

"It's going to break."

"Brenna, the branch is not going to break."

"I heard it crack."

He muttered something under his breath. Brenna didn't care. If she moved, the branch would snap. She'd smash against the wall before landing in a heap on the distant ground. Without a doubt, she'd shatter every bone in her body. She was *not* moving.

"Brenna?" He climbed toward her.

"Don't! It won't support both of us!"

She felt his fingers on her ankle, warm against her cold skin. They inched upward.

"Brenna, it's okay," he said quietly.

"No, it's not okay! The branch is going to snap!"

"Brenna, listen to me. Do you feel my hand?"

"Of course I do."

A sudden gust of wind set the entire tree swaying. Brenna hadn't known she could grip the limb more tightly. It was distinctly possible that it would require surgery to part her from this tree limb.

Spencer slid his palm across her buttock.

"What are you doing?" she gasped.

"Nothing."

"Well, stop it."

"I like touching you."

"You're completely mad!"

"Not at all." His words were calm and quiet. "Are you wearing that sexy black bra, Brenna? The one you had on the other night?" he moved further out on the swaying branch.

"What are you *doing*?"

"Shh. Keep your voice down. Sound travels at night."

From the yard next door came the faint sound of voices, carried on the wind. She'd forgotten all about the police. At least the dog had stopped barking.

Spencer suddenly gripped her waist. He'd practically climbed on the top of her and she hadn't even noticed.

"Very slowly," he whispered, "inch your way back against me."

"We'll fall."

He squeezed her. "I won't let you fall."

Strangely, the panic fled. Brenna inched backward. So did Spencer. The limb protested—loudly.

"Spen—"

"Shh!"

The tension in his voice made her look down and back. Flashlight beams danced amid the bushes. Two shadowy figures worked their way along the perimeter of the fence line. Brenna held perfectly still. So did Spencer. He gripped her waist tightly.

With excruciating slowness, the figures neared the crab apple tree. All they had to do was turn those beams of light upward and she and Spencer would be featured on the eleven o'clock news.

"Over here," one of the men called out.

They moved directly beneath the tree. Brenna held her breath. The one who called out swung his beam along the wall and stopped not four feet past the tree where a heavy wood gate had been built into the concrete.

The second man moved forward cautiously and tested the gate. "Open," he said. "If there was an intruder, and he came this way, he's long gone."

The two men peered down the street, then came back inside, barred the gate, and continued their trek along the perimeter of the yard away from the tree.

"There was a gate," Brenna hissed when their lights disappeared past the pool.

"I saw it."

"Well, why the heck didn't you see it before we climbed this blasted tree?"

"Fate? Let's get out of here."

Spencer released her and started edging backward. Brenna followed quickly. She wasn't sure, but she didn't think her heart started beating again until she reached the ground.

"Let's go."

Spencer shook his head. "No."

"What do you mean, no? Those men could come back any minute."

"Didn't you hear what they said? They aren't even sure there was a burglar. No one saw us."

"So?"

"So the last thing they'll expect is another attempt. We'll just wait until everything calms down and go back."

Even in the dark, he knew she gaped at him. "Are you crazy? Have you forgotten Killer, the rabid canine?"

"Oh. Yeah, the dog could be a problem."

"Could be?"

Spencer sighed. "Tomorrow is Sunday, Brenna. We have to get the painting tonight or tomorrow."

"I vote for tomorrow."

"They'll be even more prepared tomorrow."

He could almost hear her mind churning over that.

"I have an idea," she said. "Could we discuss it in the car?"

Spencer nodded and led the way through the gate, pulling it shut behind them. They walked back to the car.

"Okay. What's your plan?"

"I'll call and ask Hadden if we can tour the house tomorrow."

She sounded smugly pleased.

"That's it? That's your plan?"

"It's a perfectly good plan."

"It's stupid. How are we going to get the painting?"

"First we locate it, by walking through the rooms. Then I'll distract him while you slip it under your coat or something."

"That will never work."

"Well, it's better than facing Killer and his group of storm troopers. I am not climbing any more trees tonight, and if you suggest pole-vaulting I'll hurt you."

He grinned, despite himself. "No pole-vaulting, gotcha." Spencer slumped back against his seat. They'd been lucky so far. He couldn't count on their luck holding much longer.

"What we need is a distraction," he told her.

She snuggled against him. "What sort of a distraction?"

"I don't know, but I'll think of something."

Three hours later, the only distraction he could think about was the one Brenna presented as she snored softly into his shoulder. His arm had gone to sleep half an hour after she did, but he didn't have the heart to disturb her. He liked having her cuddled against him in the tight confines of the car. Unfortunately, that wasn't going to help them get the painting.

Spencer gently tugged his arm free. She woke instantly.

"What's wrong?"

"Nothing. It's getting late. Time to head home."

She gripped his tingling arm. "You are not dropping me off and coming back here later tonight."

"Actually, I wasn't planning to drop you off at all. I was hoping you'd be willing to go back to my place for what's left of the night."

She released his arm and he rubbed it, trying to restore circulation.

"What about the painting?"

"In the morning, you can call and request the grand tour." He flexed his tingling fingers. "Tell Hadden I'm looking to invest in some property. He'll save a bundle if he sells it without going through a realtor. I'll bet he'll jump at the chance."

She stared at him in darkness. "What changed your mind?"

"I keep remembering how soft your skin is."

"I'm serious."

"So am I."

She released his arm.

"Brenna?"

She leaned over, cupped his face and sought his mouth.

Spencer kissed her back. He loved the way she melted against him. A light scent clung to her hair. He loved her quick mind and quirky humor and her daring zest for life. And he loved that she was intensely passionate and not afraid to take chances.

His lips greedily devoured her. She matched his passion, kiss for kiss.

He stroked her silky hair, delighting in the texture. She ran her hands up and down his back, her breathing growing faster and faster, mingling with his.

When she gave of herself, she gave completely. She'd taken a tremendous risk for her grandfather, just as he was doing for his grandmother. No doubt she'd be equally protective of the man she loved.

The thought was sobering. He pulled back and so did she.

"Before we go back to your place, I have one question," she said breathlessly.

"What's that?"

"Which one of us is going to wear the handcuffs?"

Spencer began to laugh as Brenna reached for her seat belt.

What was not to love about this woman? A man would never be bored with her around, that was for sure. He pulled on his own seat belt and started the engine. Her hand came to rest on his thigh.

Her fingers trailed lightly up and down his pant leg.

"What are you doing?"

"Marking my place. I don't want to forget where we left off."

Her fingers brushed across his thigh dangerously close to where he most wanted them to be.

"You're a tease, you know that?"

"It's so good to be appreciated."

"Will your grandfather be upset if you don't come home tonight?"

"I think my grandfather will be disappointed if I do."

Her hand became bolder, stroking his erection.

"Well, I wouldn't want to disappoint your grandfather."

"Neither would I. Should we stop and pick up some fruit?" she joked.

He pictured the erotic painting with the fruit just as her hand closed over him.

"We are not stopping for anything," he told her.

"Good."

Spencer decided it was a miracle they made it all the way home in one piece. He made the distance from Potomac to Germantown in record time as they shared fantasies of what would happen once they reached the apartment. She had him so aroused he didn't think they'd make it inside before he exploded.

They made it to his bed by leaving a trail of clothing in their wake. Their lovemaking was wild and rollicking. Laughter mingled with the soft sounds of passion. Touching her was a subtle feast of textures and sensations. Being touched by her was exquisite.

Brenna prodded him until he rolled on his back. He allowed her to take command and she did so with the same indefatigable energy she applied to everything.

Spencer suffered gloriously as she teased and touched and kissed his body, barely letting him return the wild loving. He could see her eyes glittering with fierce pleasure, even though she'd removed his glasses.

"You're going to kill me," he warned.

She drew her mouth from him and straddled his body, running her hands over his chest. Her kiss was soul-deep, branding him forever.

"Just the little death," she promised. And she lowered herself over him with painstaking slowness.

He reached for her breasts, kneading them, tugging at her erect nipples as she began to ride him in slow deliberate torture.

"Brenna…" He couldn't find words, so he showed her with a kiss all the emotions he couldn't put into words. As their mouths fused, he gripped her strongly, moving with her as their wild frenzy reached an unbearable crescendo.

Brenna collapsed against his sweat-slicked chest, her eyes fluttering closed. He held her tenderly, sated and at peace. Sleep claimed him almost immediately.

He wakened a long time later, surprised to find his fingers cupping something soft and round and firm. Brenna lay curled spoon-style against him. It felt so natural. So right. His hand slid over her rib cage, tracing a path downward. She stirred and opened one sleepy eye.

"Again?" she whispered.

He reached the junction of her thighs. "Not if you don't want."

Her legs parted to give him access. "Who says I don't want?"

Their loving was slow this time, infinitely tender. And afterward, he cradled her against his body while he came to grips with the idea that he'd fallen in love with Brenna Wolford.

SPENCER WOKE TO THE scent of coffee, unhappy to find his arms empty. Brenna bustled around in his kitchen singing off-key along with the radio.

Spencer grinned. He reached for his glasses and found his clothing in a neat pile on the end of the bed. He snatched a clean outfit from his closet and headed for the bathroom. Half an hour later, shaved and dressed, he wandered into the kitchen to find Brenna taking bacon from the oven.

"Good morning," she greeted.

He waited until she set the hot pan down and then went over and kissed her soundly. "Good morning," he responded when he finally let her go. "Where did you find bacon? And bagels?" he added as he noted the table set for two.

"Some of us aren't slugabeds," she told him, turning back to the bacon. "I took your car keys and ran to the store."

"My stomach thanks you most humbly." He reached for the coffee pot and filled his cup.

"I also called Hadden. We have an appointment to see the house in two hours."

Spencer paused, the coffee cup halfway to his lips. "What did you tell him?"

"I told him I had a friend who was really curious about all the artwork and might even be interested in buying the place. I asked if we could take an unofficial tour and he said yes. He and Kerry aren't going to be home, but he left word with the housekeeper. Anna is going to show us around."

"I don't believe it."

Smugly, she sat down and lifted her own coffee cup. "I only wish I'd thought of this last Friday before we risked getting caught sneaking inside. We'll locate the painting then I'll distract Anna and you can sneak it out under your sweater or something."

"Brenna—"

"On second thought, I'll bring that big canvas tote bag and we can stick it in there."

"Brenna—"

"Don't worry about a distraction, I'll come up with something. I'm good at distractions."

He grinned. "I know you are."

They exchanged looks that should have set fire on the placemats.

"You are beautiful, intelligent and sexy as hell," he added. Then he nodded toward the object still lying in the middle of the table. "And we are definitely going to try out these handcuffs. I want to see you chained to my bed so I can do all these things to you that you did to me last night."

She looked down at the handcuffs. "Now?" she asked weakly.

"Not now. Tonight. After my grandmother's party."

Her head came up, her expression stricken. "I won't be here tonight."

"What are you talking about."

"I have a nine o'clock flight out of National Airport. I have to be at work tomorrow."

"What?"

"I don't live here, Spencer. I thought I explained that I live in New York.

"Damn." He couldn't believe it. She was planning to leave. "What about us? It's going to be a little hard for us to have a relationship if you live in New York and I live in Maryland."

Brenna wouldn't meet his eyes. Her gaze roved about his kitchen. "Maybe that's just as well. I'm not very good at relationships, Spencer."

"What's that supposed to mean?"

"My mother is working on husband number six."

Completely puzzled, he stared at her as her fingers set about shredding a paper napkin. "So?"

"So I take after her."

"You've been married six times?"

Her eyes flashed angrily. "Of course not. I've never been married."

"Well, good."

"You don't understand."

He covered her hand, making her fingers stop their destruction. "Okay. Help me here, Brenna. What's going on?"

Her chin lifted and her jaw jutted forward. "I haven't found a relationship that's lasted beyond the initial attraction," she said stubbornly.

"Neither have I."

She eyed him suspiciously. "What do you want from me?" And when he smiled, she glared and pulled her hand back. "Besides sex."

Spencer answered her seriously. "A chance to get to know you. A chance to see if we have something in common besides our grandparents' connection to an old painting. For example, what do you do in New York?"

"I'm a planning analyst."

"I don't suppose you could be a planning analyst here?

Brenna sat up straighter in her chair. Her chin came up and he knew he'd pushed another wrong button.

"I happen to like my job, Spencer. It is a very good job that pays well. Why don't you consider moving? I'm sure there's a big market for thieves in New York."

He refused to be decoyed by her defensive reactions. He swallowed a tasteless bite of something and set down his fork. "I'm an engineer."

"See? New York is filled with engineers."

"I'm in line to be partner at my firm one day, Brenna."

She picked up her fork and set it back down again. "So you're saying your job is more important than mine?"

Spencer shook his head. "Nope. We were sharing information. That's what getting to know one another is all about."

Brenna looked down at her plate. "The last man I dated was seriously appalled that I would leave the D.C. area to take a huge promotion in New York."

Spencer heard a wealth of insecurities underlying those words. Those insecurities only made her more appealing.

"Too bad I didn't know you then. We could have introduced him to the last woman I dated. She expected a ring after the third date." He sat back and smiled easily. "I wanted to know her a little better and she was planning children."

"So you aren't looking for marriage and children?"

He thought about the fact that Brenna could, even now, be pregnant with his child. Given an option, he'd wait. If there wasn't one, well, the idea thrilled instead of chilled him. "The idea is sort of nice—with the right woman. How about you?"

Brenna frowned. "I never gave it much serious thought. Watching my mother jump from one husband to another..." Her shoulders rose and fell in a shrug.

"What about your father?"

"He's been married three times. Of course, his first wife died and then he married my mother."

"And his current wife?"

"They've been married thirteen years," she admitted grudgingly.

"And your grandfather was married all his life to your grandmother."

Her expression sharpened dangerously. "I know you're not asking me to marry you, Spencer. So why are we having this conversation?"

He reached for her hand again, this time not letting her pull it back. "I'm just asking for a chance to get to know you. I don't want to throw this relationship away until we see where it leads.

She stared at their hands before meeting his expression. "Me neither, but I have to be at my desk tomorrow, Spencer."

"So do I."

She looked as miserable as he felt. "So what are we going to do?"

"I don't know. Let's start with finding the painting."

THEY TOURED the Summerton estate from bottom to top. B. J. Wolford's work was represented in several rooms, from a couple of small paintings in the dining room to a large scene in the hall upstairs. There were plenty of nudes scattered throughout the mansion, but none of them depicted Spencer's grandmother.

Brenna slumped against the car seat in utter dejection as they left the estate. "Maybe it's tucked away in a drawer somewhere, or in the big safe in the library," she said morosely. "Canvas can be rolled, you know, and this one isn't very large."

"Even if we had free access to the house, we couldn't search every nook and cranny. Did Hadden have another house or a boat, maybe an office somewhere?" Spencer asked.

"No. What are we going to do? The appraisers will arrive first thing in the morning."

"I know."

Spencer felt as bad as Brenna. Once the public eye was focused on that painting, it wouldn't take long before someone would connect his grandmother's well-known face to the subject. Particularly with national coverage of the anti-child pornography campaign in two weeks.

He ground his teeth in frustration. Brenna stared in gloomy silence out the window at the passing scenery. There was nothing more either of them could do.

"Brenna, I'm sorry I implied your job was less important than mine. I didn't mean it."

"I know." Her voice took on a wistful tone. "I only got angry because Todd couldn't believe I'd choose a job over him."

Jealousy stirred in his chest. "He meant something to you?"

"He was a nice person," Brenna hedged.

Spencer relaxed. A woman didn't describe someone she felt passionate about as nice. "Am I a 'nice' person?"

Her lips quirked upward. "Occasionally. How do you want to be considered?"

"Oh, sexy, fascinating, intelligent—"

"Can you get a hat on over that ego?"

"Never wear 'em."

"Figures." But she was smiling again.

"I've got some errands to run before my grandmother's dinner party tonight. I'll pick you up around five-thirty."

Brenna twisted to face him. "I can't come."

"Why not? Your plane isn't until nine."

"Spencer, I want to spend a couple of hours with my grandfather before I leave. This next week is going to be really hard on him."

He swallowed disappointment. "Okay. I understand. Maybe I can fly to New York next weekend."

"I'd like that," she agreed softly.

"And there's always the telephone."

"Obscene calls?" she teased.

"Lewdly erotic. Filled with indecent suggestions of a lustful nature."

"Are you sure those sex toys belonged to your sister?"

"Want to go try out the handcuffs?"

Her smile bloomed, easing the tension in his chest. "Maybe. Eventually."

11

BRENNA STUDIED his grandmother's gracious brick home in a quiet area in Chevy Chase, and wondered what Spencer would say when he saw her. She'd arrived back at her grandfather's only to find him in a tizzy because they'd both been invited to Regina's dinner party. She tried to call Spencer to let him know about the change of plans, but couldn't reach him. No doubt Regina had told him they were coming.

Brenna had never seen her grandfather quite this excited before. Now, as he parked the car on the street outside Regina's house, he stepped on the sidewalk and immediately straightened his tie.

"You're sure I look okay?" he asked Brenna for the third time.

She kept her twitching lips under control. He was endearingly nervous. "You look dashing."

"You wouldn't lie to an old man, now, would you?" he asked as they walked up the porch steps.

"Probably, but in this case I don't have to. You'll bowl her over."

"That's not exactly what I had in mind," he said ruefully.

And then they were at the door and Brenna's own butterflies took wing. How was she going to face Spencer's grandmother after the insane way she'd behaved on the telephone earlier? And what would Spencer think when he saw her there? Would he be alone, or would he have another date? The thought was surprisingly painful.

Spencer opened the door, incredibly handsome in a dark suit and tie, his expression warmly welcoming. An answering excitement hummed through her.

He smiled wickedly. "You're late."

"We are not. We're two minutes early. And how did you know we were coming?"

"I wished for it on a pair of handcuffs," he whispered in her ear as he helped her off with her coat. "And how are you this evening, Mr. Wolford?" he asked her grandfather.

Brenna was pretty sure her grandfather hadn't even heard the question. She followed his stare to find Regina Griffen gliding forward with ageless grace and beauty. Brenna would have recognized her anywhere.

"Regina," her grandfather breathed.

"Benji?"

Brenna had never heard her grandfather called Benji before. And she'd never seen such a smitten expression on his face before either. The two of them had obviously forgotten she and Spencer were standing in the hall.

Spencer caught her eye and grinned. "Brenna, may I present my grandmother, Regina Griffen?"

Regina seemed to come out of her own daze. She smiled with hospitable charm and extended a dainty hand. "So nice to finally meet you in person, my dear. I enjoyed our earlier conversation immensely." She winked at Brenna to show she was teasing.

Brenna blushed, liking the woman at once.

"Do come inside, everyone. It's grown quite chilly outside."

As informal host for his grandmother, Spencer seldom remained in one spot for long, but Brenna came to look forward to his small touches and intimate glances whenever he came near her. In a room that seemed full of people, there was a powerful connection between them.

Dinner for twelve was laid out at a long formal table. Neither end of the table was set. Regina sat near the center of the table, Brenna's grandfather on one side, a senator on the other. Spencer sat across from his grandmother with Brenna on his right and a well-known film star on his left. All of the prestigious guests were supporters of Regina's anti–child pornography campaign.

With such an eclectic group of people, conversations touched on all sorts of topics. Brenna found herself relaxing and thoroughly enjoying the evening, until she caught the gist of the conversation the doctor across the table was having with Spencer.

"Well, more power to the two of you if you can make it work," the woman said, with a toss of her head. "There's no such thing as a fifty-fifty relationship. Someone is always going to have to give more at different times than the other. Add distance to the mix, and both of you will have to make a serious effort."

"Brenna's worth it," Spencer replied warmly.

The congressman on her right asked Brenna to pass the butter, drawing her attention away from the troubling conversation. The doctor had an excellent point. How could Brenna and Spencer have a meaningful relationship living so many miles apart? Sooner or later, the distance would become a serious issue.

Brenna nearly jumped when a sock-clad foot suddenly slid disturbingly along her ankle and up her stockinged calf. Up and down it traveled in suggestive strokes.

"Stop that," she whispered to Spencer when she got a chance.

"I'm sorry, Brenna, did you say something?" he asked innocently.

She kicked his shin and smiled when he winced. "Would you pass the pepper, please?"

"Certainly." As he handed it to her, he managed to caress the back of her hand.

She added the unwanted pepper to her salad and resumed her conversation with the congressman and his wife. Minutes later, Spencer's hand brushed the top of her thigh, stroking the silk of her dress. She nearly leaped out of her seat.

"Is something wrong, my dear?" Regina inquired.

"Just a small muscle spasm," she replied without looking at Spencer. "I did several foolish and unfamiliar activities this weekend—climbing and that sort of thing."

"Oh, did you climb Sugarloaf Mountain?" someone asked. "My son takes his children up there all the time. The view is quite spectacular. Particularly when the trees are at their peak."

Brenna gave a noncommittal answer and let the conversation swirl around her as she plotted her revenge. Unfortunately, nothing suitable presented itself as the evening sped past and guests began to leave.

Finally, it was just the four of them in the spacious living room, lingering over coffee and conversation when Spencer suddenly stood.

"Brenna, you missed your plane!"

"I changed flights," she told him calmly. "I'm flying back at seven-fifteen in the morning instead of tonight."

Spencer dropped back down on the couch, so close to her that his thigh pressed hers. His smile was warm with promise. "Good."

"Yes. Grandpa and I have hardly had any time together this weekend. I thought I'd make the most of this evening."

Spencer's expression promised retribution. He knew exactly what she was doing. The subtle game of teasing at the dinner table had heightened their mutual awareness, even though both knew the evening wouldn't end with them together.

Brenna leaned back, comfortably aware of Spencer at her side as the two of them listened to their grandparents reminisce. Finally, the conversation came around to the missing painting.

"Regina, I've owed you an apology for fifty years," her grandfather said suddenly. "I should never have sold that painting."

"No, you shouldn't have, but I forgave you a long time ago. My share of that money enabled me to go back to school," she smiled to include her listeners. "That's where I met Spencer's grandfather." She turned back to B. J. Wolford. "Besides, the sale gave you the money to continue with your career, and it let Hadden begin a most profitable venture. I just hate to think your career could be destroyed if the forgery comes to light."

Her grandfather snorted. "It'll probably gain me notoriety and send my prices skyrocketing." He leaned across the end table and covered Regina's hand with his own. "You needn't worry. I'll be fine. And I will deny that you were the model. If pressed, I will admit I had a crush on you and used your face over my model's figure."

"Don't be ridiculous."

"I'm quite serious, Regina. Nothing will harm your reputation or interfere with the work you've been doing over the past few years."

Spencer stood, tugging on Brenna's hand. "Brenna,

would you help me with something out in the kitchen for a minute?" he asked.

"Now, dear, the cleaning service will be back first thing in the morning," his grandmother said, briefly diverted.

"I know. I just want to talk to Brenna for a second. If you'll excuse us?"

Brenna followed him to the kitchen. "What did you need?" she asked.

"This."

Brenna found herself shoved back against the refrigerator door while Spencer kissed the breath from her body.

"Fool," she panted when he finally released her. "Your grandmother could walk in here any minute."

"Not if your grandfather is half the man I think he is."

He fondled her breast through the silk of her dress.

"Spencer! You're talking about our grandparents!"

"Yep. Let's not waste time talking."

He inserted his leg between hers, his mouth covering her lips again with a hunger she easily matched.

It would be so easy to love this man, she thought, as she felt his lips on the sensitive skin of her neck.

"Don't go," he whispered.

And she knew he was talking about her plane ride in the morning.

"I have to." She stroked the bulge she felt hidden behind his fly and kissed him deeply, tasting the coffee and a touch of mint from dessert.

She didn't want to leave in the morning. They needed time to see if there was something more enduring than this incredible, mind-boggling sex behind their wild attraction. Unfortunately, she had an obligation to her employers.

"Let me take you to the airport," he asked. His

thumb erotically rubbed the tip of her breast through the material of her dress and bra.

"I have to leave by six," she answered, stroking his back, pressing him more tightly against her.

"I'll pick you up at five-thirty. We can have breakfast together at the airport." His hand slid under her full skirt, skimming up over the silken hose.

"No one eats at five-thirty in the morning." She squeezed the hardness of his erection, gratified by the low sound he made deep in his throat.

His eyes sparkled with mischief. "Oh, I don't know." He nibbled at her neck. "I can think of a few choice items I'd be willing to sample at any hour." His fingers rubbed her through the pantyhose.

Brenna nipped at his earlobe.

And her grandfather cleared his throat in the dining room. They sprang apart guiltily as he called out, "You two scrubbing the pots and pans, or what? You know, you've got a plane to catch in a couple of hours, Brenna."

"I'll be right there." Her voice only shook a little when she answered him. Spencer grinned at her like a fool.

Regina's voice began scolding. "Oh, leave them alone, Benji. I can remember when we were their age. Remember the time you pushed me into the broom closet at my…" Her voice trailed away as she must have led the older man back into the hall.

"A broom closet?" Spencer asked on a chuckle. "Now why didn't I think of that?"

"They don't have broom closets anymore," Brenna told him primly, straightening her dress. "Modern women use vacuum cleaners."

"Very funny. Your lipstick's gone."

"No, it isn't. You're wearing it."

Spencer wiped at his mouth as she chuckled. They

straightened their clothing before they rejoined the older couple in the hall near the front door.

Brenna knew their grandparents were sure to notice her swollen lips from Spencer's kisses and the sudden absence of her lipstick, but she suspected they wouldn't be surprised. Besides, there was nothing she could do about it now.

"Spencer offered to take me to the airport, Grandpa," she announced.

Her grandfather stared at her face for just a moment before nodding sagely. Regina Linnington winked at her, and Brenna knew that she flushed. Brenna and her grandfather said their good-nights and Spencer insisted on walking them to the car. He placed a chaste kiss on her forehead under her grandfather's watchful eyes and waited for her to climb inside. She saw him watching until they drove out of sight.

"Planning to marry him?" her grandfather asked.

"We just met!"

"Hmph. Well, don't keep him dangling too long. I'd like to see some great-grandkids while I'm young enough to spoil 'em."

"Grandpa!"

"He's a good man, Brenna. I like him."

"So do I."

"YO, SPENCE. Hey, man, don't you know you were off the clock an hour ago?"

Spencer raised his eyes from his computer terminal to find his co-worker, Stu, standing in his doorway. He nodded absently. "Just checking these numbers before tomorrow's meeting."

"They're right on and you know it. What's got you so uptight lately? You need to unwind, man. How about a game of handball?"

"Not tonight."

Stu pushed aside a stack of papers and perched on the edge of the desk.

"Hey, don't mess those up," Spencer protested.

His co-worker gazed pointedly around the paper-strewn office. "Look, I know a couple of women who are looking for something to do tomorrow night. What do you say we take them to see that new action-adventure movie?"

Spencer shut off his machine and shook his head. "No, but thanks for asking."

"Listen, man, I gotta tell you, you look like hell lately."

Stu's round, pudgy face grew somber. "You been working the past few weeks like you're in line for a major promotion any day now. What gives?"

Spencer was tempted to tell him. The last four weeks and three days of his life had revolved around telephone calls until two in the morning, weekends when he'd ride the shuttle back and forth to New York, and hours spent planning the next weekend to come. Work was his only refuge from obsessive thoughts of Brenna. He knew it was ridiculous, but there didn't seem to be anything he could do about it. The darn woman had him bewitched. He found himself making excuses to clear his social calendar. The two dates he did keep were close to disasters. Jolie and Liz were both nice women, but they simply weren't Brenna.

Brenna was funny and intelligent and so easy to be with. The weekends weren't long enough.

The appraisers had finished at the Hadden estate. But if the nude and forgery had been discovered, no one spoke of it. The waiting was killing all four of them.

"Spence? Are you listening to me?"

"What? Sorry, Stu, I was just thinking."

Stu's dark eyes gleamed. "If I didn't know better I'd say it was woman trouble."

"Why do you say that?"

"You've got all the symptoms."

"No, I mean, why do you say if you didn't know better?"

"Spencer, we've worked together what, almost two years now? I've watched you play the field with an ease I'd kill to emulate. All of a sudden, you aren't interested. The new girl, Cindy, she's practically drooling over you and you haven't even noticed her—and man, that woman is worth a second look. Either some woman has you tied in knots, or you've got a serious problem here, buddy."

Spencer stared at Stu. He could easily picture the voluptuous Cindy, but her image only reminded him that he needed the Vasquez report back from her. He was tied in knots all right. He stood and reached for his briefcase. "You're right."

"Damn straight, I'm right." Stu pushed off the desk and bent to retrieve some fallen papers. "Right about what?"

"She's got me tied in knots."

"You mean, it is a woman?"

Spencer smiled, but he didn't answer the question directly. "Is that sexy lingerie shop still at the mall?"

Stu's mouth gaped open comically.

"Never mind." He saw that his job résumé was still sitting on his desk and casually covered the papers with some correspondence. Stu liked to gossip. No sense in giving the man anything to speculate about.

"I think you've flipped out, Spence."

"You may be right. See you tomorrow."

The specialty shop was still at the mall. Spencer shopped, then stopped at a restaurant for a late dinner before heading home. He sure wished he could be a fly on the wall at Brenna's office the next day.

"HELLO?" SHE ANSWERED her telephone, somewhat breathlessly, a few hours later.

Spencer lay back against his bed, the telephone held to his ear. "Did I catch you at an interesting moment?" Her voice filled him with a wash of pleasure, as always.

"Actually, I was thinking of you."

He liked that idea. Liked it a lot. "Really?"

"Yes."

"What are you wearing?"

Brenna hesitated, obviously surprised by his question.

"I did tell you I'd make an obscene phone call to you if you liked, remember?" he teased.

"I remember."

"Do you want to tell me what you're wearing?"

"I...don't think so."

"Are you naked?" He could picture her naked, all wet from a shower, beads of moisture running across her skin.

"Not completely."

He groaned and changed the picture to that black lace bra he liked so much.

"Actually, I was trying on a merry widow."

"What's a merry widow?"

Laughter quickened in her voice. "I'll show you this weekend. You're going to like it."

"Is it black?"

"No. It's red—to match your sheets."

"Sounds promising," he told her. "I'm going to fly in a bit earlier this week."

"No. I'm coming to D.C. for the weekend."

"You are?"

"Yes. Kerry called me today. Hadden is hosting an informal open house this weekend for his grandfather's clients and friends. Whatever isn't sold to them is going up for public auction three weeks from Saturday."

Spencer sat up against the headboard and pushed his glasses back against the bridge of his nose. His grandmother's campaign had gone off without a hitch a couple of weeks ago. If that damn painting came to light now....

"We're invited to attend the open house. *Everything* is being displayed, Spencer. *Nothing* is being held back."

"The nude?"

"Kerry didn't know much about any of the individual pieces, but she assures me the auditors went through every single item in the estate. Hadden is anxious to sell off the contents, pay the back taxes, and unload the mausoleum, as he calls it."

"What time is your flight?"

"I'm going to take the train. There's one around five-thirty."

"I'll pick you up."

"Okay. I haven't been able to reach my grandfather tonight anyhow."

"They're at the Kennedy Center Opera House."

"My grandfather hates opera."

"My grandmother loves it." Spencer grinned and heard Brenna giggle.

"This is getting serious. I think they used to be lovers," Brenna told him.

"I expect so. I didn't think she posed for him just because he asked."

"She might have."

"You don't know my grandmother."

"They'll be at the private showing. Grandpa was invited as one of Hadden's friends and clients."

"Good. The two of them can help us look for that damn painting."

"I think Hadden already destroyed it, Spencer."

"Well, if so, I wish he had told someone. He could have saved us an awful lot of grief."

"We would never have met without it," she reminded him.

Spencer removed his glasses and lay back down. "There is that. I gather you don't make a habit of hiding under other people's beds?"

"No more than you do climbing trees and breaking into other people's houses."

"Touché. Do you think we can get your friend Hadden to let us play in his grandfather's bathroom for a couple of hours?"

"You have a dirty mind."

"Thank you. Describe a merry widow."

"A widow who laughs a lot." Amusement laced her voice. "You'll see it this weekend."

"That's two whole days from now."

"I know. But it will give you something to dream about."

"I'd rather dream about you, covered in whipped cream and strawberries."

"Strawberries?" she asked weakly.

"Hmm, how about shaved chocolate? The berries would probably fall off," he said. "Are you laughing?"

"Heavens no. Do you have a fruit fetish I should be aware of?"

"Only when it involves you. Will you dream of me?"

"Always."

Spencer replaced the receiver slowly and stared at

the ceiling. In the past weeks they'd discussed so many things, often into the early morning hours.

He had a much better understanding of her past and the insecurities that stemmed from a mother who loved too often and unwisely. Brenna wanted commitment in her life, yet she was afraid to take chances with her heart. Spencer was pretty sure she feared being like her mother. She clung to her independence like a talisman.

He looked at the New York newspaper lying beside his nightstand. The help wanted section stared up at him. He wondered what Brenna would say when she got his gift tomorrow.

12

THERE WAS A SUBTLE knock on the conference room door. Brenna looked up, relieved by the interruption. The meeting had dragged on since lunch and all she could think about was the coming weekend. Irene, her friend and co-worker, stuck her head inside the room.

"Brenna? Excuse the interruption, but I need to see you right away."

Brenna excused herself and followed Irene outside. "What's up?"

Irene's broad face erupted in a giggle and she pushed aside a strand of wiry dark hair. "You wouldn't believe me if I told you." She waved her arm in the direction of Brenna's office. Several people clustered around the doorway—tittering.

Brenna's heart began to beat a little faster. "What's going on?"

"I thought you might want to get this delivery out of sight before one of the head honchos comes through the office," Irene said around another giggle.

"What delivery?"

Brenna pushed past the two people blocking her way and stopped dead. She blinked, but the sight didn't go away. A colorful spray of strange-looking balloons tied with bright ribbons were attached to a large box with the name of an exotic lingerie company prominently displayed on the top and sides.

"No wonder you didn't like any of the men I tried to

set you up with," Irene said. "You've been holdin' out on me, girl. Condom balloons? Nice touch."

Brenna gaped. "I didn't know condoms came in all those colors."

Irene laughed, her chins quivering. "Are you going to open that box?"

Not here, she wasn't. "No. Can we hide it someplace?"

"Sure, but how are you planning to get it home on the subway tonight?"

Heat flamed Brenna's cheeks. Irene was right. Brenna couldn't walk down the street carrying that box, let alone a bouquet of colored condoms.

"I'll kill him."

"Let me meet him first," Irene pleaded. "How about if we take it into McGregor's office? You can take out whatever's inside the box and stuff it in your briefcase. I'll get Harry to take the condoms and the box down to the Dumpster. Unless you want to keep them?"

"Yes. No!" How could Spencer embarrass her like this?

They hurried to McGregor's office, but not without several comments from fellow workers. She knew her face was scarlet. If only she could cancel the bonsai tree she'd sent him this morning. Had she known about this, she would have hung him in effigy from the bottom branch first. She'd sent him the tree to remind him of the way they kept finding themselves in trees. She could just imagine what Spencer planned to remind her of with this gift.

Inside lay a sheer white negligee, crotchless white satin panties, a white garter belt and sheer stockings with seams. There was also a pair of high-heeled white satin slippers.

Her guess would have been right.

"Oh, my," Irene gasped. "This boy does have some

plans. I haven't been this excited since Darius bought us that vibrator to try. Isn't that a wedding garter on the bottom there?"

Brenna picked up the satin-encased bit of elastic with trembling hands. Definitely the sort of garter brides wore on their wedding day. Was this just part of the seductive outfit, or did it have some deeper significance?

"Hon, I'm just dying to hear all the juicy details, and I don't mean to rush you, but shouldn't you be getting back to that meeting?"

"Oh, God, I forgot all about it."

"I don't blame you one bit. This is the sort of gift to make you forget everything except the sender," Irene said.

Killing would be too good for him. Slow torture. It was the only answer.

Brenna called Spencer's apartment as soon as she got home, but his answering machine picked up. She couldn't think of anything pithy enough to say, so she didn't leave a message.

By nine o'clock she kept staring at the outfit draped neatly on the chair in her bedroom, wondering if he was home and just not answering his phone. Finally, she walked over and touched the sheer material. Giving in to impulse, she donned the scanty bits of fabric. The results made her shiver. She stared at her reflection feeling sensual and naughty.

The telephone rang, startling her. She hesitated, embarrassed—a totally silly reaction since the person on the other end couldn't possibly know how she was dressed.

"Did you get my present?" Spencer's deep, sexy voice washed over her. "I got yours."

"You are a dead man."

"Ah, then you did get the present."

"You sent it to my office!"

"I couldn't have them leave it in the hall of your apartment building. It would have been gone before you got home. Besides, all your neighbors would talk. Did you like it?"

She took a deep breath.

"I can't wait to see you in it," he cajoled.

"Too bad you aren't here now."

"You're kidding, right? You're wearing it now?"

Brenna didn't answer. Spencer made a low sound that could have been a groan.

"You're killing me, you know that?" he said finally.

"I would have this afternoon if you'd been in strangling distance."

He chuckled.

"What did you think of the balloons?" he asked.

"They were perverted."

She could hear a smile in his voice. "Glad you liked them. I miss you."

The warmth in his tone soothed and comforted her, as always. "I miss you too," she told him truthfully.

"Will you dream of me?"

As if she had a choice.

"I dream of you all the time," he told her. "I picture you dressed in that outfit lying against my red satin sheets."

A new tension invaded her. "Locked in padded handcuffs?" she attempted to tease.

"Hold that thought. I'll add it tonight. I have another surprise for you, but not until I see you in person. Sleep well, Brenna."

Brenna hung up and slowly began to remove the outfit he'd sent. So he had another surprise, did he? After this one, she was afraid to imagine what it would be. She folded the bits of nylon carefully, placing them in her suitcase.

She had a surprise for him too. She'd decided to catch an early flight right after her morning meeting instead of waiting to take the train after work. That way they'd have more time together.

As she finished packing, she worried over the strength of the bond they were forging. Spencer had never told her he loved her. But she'd never said the words either. Was she allowing her mother's flighty behavior to rule her actions? She wasn't her mother and never had been. In truth, she took after her father and her grandfather.

Life didn't come with any guarantees. Spencer was fun and laughter, but he was also serious and goal-oriented. They had more than a few things in common and enjoyed sparring over their differences. In some ways, they complemented one another. She genuinely liked being with Spencer.

Brenna slipped into bed, fingering the wedding garter. This bit of nylon and lace probably meant nothing at all, except that it went with the rest of the outfit. On the other hand, maybe Spencer was showing her in subtle ways that he wanted a commitment. After all, he'd flown to New York every weekend since they'd met and he called her every night before bed. They talked themselves hoarse about everything and nothing, until they had to hang up in exhaustion so they could go to work the next day.

Spencer was intelligent. He was handsome. He was comforting and comfortable.

And she loved him.

The thought scared her to death.

Her insecurities were eating her alive because she didn't know for sure how he felt. She knew he'd stopped seeing other women. When did he have time? But was that because their relationship was still new, or because he wanted something deeper?

Brenna gripped the satin garter. The next move was up to her. Did she have the courage to take a major gamble with her life?

"I'M IRENE DUNCAN, Ms. Wolford's assistant. May I help you?"

Spencer twisted away from the reception desk to face the chunky woman with the wide, friendly face. She looked at him questioningly, brushing at a strand of her hair; he tried to curb his growing frustration. "As I told her," he said indicating the receptionist, "I'm looking for Brenna."

"I'm sorry, sir. Ms. Wolford is gone for the weekend."

"That's what the receptionist said, but Brenna isn't taking the train until this evening."

The round face split in a sudden smile. "You must be the source of the condoms and the sexy nightgown."

Heat scaled his neck. The woman studied him like a chocoholic in front of a slab of fudge.

"She's been holding out on me, big time."

"Ah, look, never mind, Irene, was it? I'll just swing by her apartment. I probably just missed her."

"By about two hours, I'd say," Irene agreed. "Her plane was at one-forty."

"She isn't flying. She's taking the commuter train this evening."

"Nope. She decided to leave early to surprise someone." The woman's eyes twinkled and she giggled. "Surprise!"

Two hours later, waiting in line to board his own plane back home, he still couldn't believe it. But at least now he was seeing the wry humor of the situation. He'd planned to surprise her and the surprise was on him. Brenna would be frantic. He'd tried to call her without success. He rubbed a thumb over his briefcase thoughtfully. Well, at least he'd gotten what he came for. More, actually. And Brenna would be waiting for him in Maryland.

The plane was overbooked, and then they had technical difficulties so his flight was delayed three hours. He arrived at National, tired and gritty. Despite being anxious to see Brenna, he resisted the impulse to head directly to her grandfather's. First he needed a shower and a change of clothing. Naturally, there was a wreck on the parkway, so he sat in traffic another forty-five minutes while the police cleared the road.

He'd tried to reach Brenna several more times, but never got an answer. As soon as stores opened in the morning, he was going to buy her grandfather an answering machine.

Spencer showered quickly and changed into jeans and a shirt and sweater. Just before going out the door, his gaze landed on the pair of handcuffs sitting on the end table. Another one of those crazy ideas flashed into his head.

He was having a lot of crazy ideas lately, he thought, picking up the handcuffs with a sudden smile, and Brenna might be making him crazy, but he didn't mind a bit— it was a fun sort of crazy.

Lights glowed softly in her grandfather's living room and nothing moved inside. Spencer eyed her dark bedroom window. Smiling to himself, he walked to the curb and selected a few choice stones.

His first two attempts at her window were way off the mark, skittering down the roof to land in the gutter. The third stone landed with a soft ping against the glass. He was ready to lob his final stone when the front door opened.

"What the hell's going on out here? Spencer? That you?"

Guiltily, Spencer dropped the last rock to face B. J. Wolford.

"Uh, yes sir. That is, I'm sorry. I was just trying—"

"Oh, I can *see* what you were trying." The older shook his head. "Doorbell stopped working?"

"Er, no, sir. That is, I didn't want to risk waking you, it's so late and all."

"It certainly is. She went to bed mad as a wet hen when you didn't show up and you didn't call. You'd better have a terrific explanation."

"I do." Spencer stepped into the hall and her grandfather's steely gray eyes pinned him where he stood. Then they landed on the handcuffs in his left hand. Embarrassed, Spencer could only meet the older man's stare and ignore the red heat seeping into his cheeks.

"You just might need those handcuffs to make her sit still and listen."

Spencer relaxed. Her grandfather was on his side. And Brenna wouldn't be in a temper unless she cared. "I hope you don't mind, but I came to kidnap her."

The corners of his eyes gained a new set of crinkles. "Well, do it quietly, will you, boy? I'm trying to read."

"Yes, sir." He nearly sighed in relief before starting up the stairs.

"Her door's at the end of the hall," her grandfather added. "You are planning to marry her, aren't you?"

"Yes, sir...eventually...when she's had time to get used to the idea."

B. J. Wolford's lips started to curl upwards. He cleared his throat. "See that you do. She has a mind of her own."

"That she does."

The older man nodded and allowed a small smile. "Good luck. You're going to need it."

"Thank you, sir. Good night."

Spencer took the rest of the stairs in twos. He liked her grandfather. And it was nice to know he had one person on his side.

Outside her door, he paused. There was no sound from inside. He eased it open and stepped into the dark room. His foot came down on something soft and squishy. He bent and lifted the small item, discovering the wedding garter in his hand.

Uh-oh. Not a good sign. She *could* have simply dropped it, but knowing Brenna, she probably threw it at the door in a fit of temper.

Damn. He wouldn't have deliberately hurt her for anything. He walked to the bed and softly called her name. She didn't move. Her hair lay in tangles about her head, spilling across the pillow in a tempting display. Gently, he laid a hand on her shoulder.

With a shriek of fear, she rolled across the bed, coming off on the other side, her hand groping for her nightstand.

"Brenna—"

He ducked as a book missed his head by inches and sailed across the room, slamming against the wall at his back.

"Brenna, it's me!"

She hesitated, her arm drawn back to throw the next item. "Spencer?"

"Yes. Who the hell did you think I was?"

She lowered her arm, but not her voice. "The burglar who's been terrorizing the area recently. I should have known you were him."

He came around the bed. "I am *not* a burglar."

"Then what are you doing, sneaking in here in the dead of night?" She backed up, still holding the large object in her hand.

"It's only a little after midnight. I came for you." She wore a long T-shirt that stopped mid-thigh. He eyed the long expanse of her legs and wondered if she had anything on underneath. "Put your weapon down."

"No. I'm mad at you."

"I know you are." He moved closer. "I'm mad at me too. I wanted to be here a lot sooner. Are you going to let me explain or are you going to hit me with that lamp?"

She lowered her arm. "That depends. Where have you been?"

He had no intention of discussing his trip to New York until he was more certain of her mood. He reached out and plucked the lamp from her hand, setting it on the tabletop. "I was out of town and my plane was delayed."

"You couldn't call?"

The handcuffs dangled at his side, out of sight. "I tried to call. No one answered. Your grandfather doesn't have an answering machine."

"He does too."

"Well, it wasn't on."

She spotted the handcuffs then and tried to back away.

"What do you think you're going to do with those?"

He didn't miss the way her breathing quickened, or the excited awareness that suddenly charged the atmosphere between them. Her eyes glittered like two dark gemstones, but it was her lack of fear that gave him courage.

"Hold out your wrists, Brenna."

"Don't even think about it," she warned, dancing back out of reach until she came up against the dresser.

"Come here."

"No!" She feinted to one side. Spencer caught her hand and clicked the cuff into place.

"What do you think you're doing?" She twisted away from him.

"Kidnapping you again. Now hold still."

"No." And she kicked him in the shin.

"If you'd had shoes on that would have hurt," he told her.

"I'll be sure and wear some next time."

Her manacled hand accidentally caught him in the mouth as he reached for her and she attempted to twist away. Spencer got the other cuff on her wrist, holding her against his body.

"Take these off me. I'm not kidding, Spencer."

She aimed another well-placed kick, but he stepped back to avoid it, spotting her suitcase on the floor.

"Later. Now behave."

"Not a chance."

Their eyes met and held. Damn. She was so vulnerable. His lips covered hers, gently insistent. Brenna froze, letting him kiss her, but not responding.

"All day," he said quietly, "all I could think about was getting to you. Each delay, each frustration, made me just a little crazier, because there was nothing I could do to speed things up and I knew you'd be worried. I want you, Brenna. So damn much."

This time when his lips covered hers, she flowed against him, parting her lips tentatively to taste him.

Spencer heaved a mental sigh of relief. Everything was going to be all right. She might be angry, but she still wanted him. That was a start. He released her slowly.

"I'm still not going anywhere with you," she announced.

"Want to bet?" He scooped her over his shoulder.

Brenna wriggled. "Put me down or you'll sing soprano for the rest of your life."

He gave her fanny a light swat. "Stop struggling unless you want me to drop you." He reached for her suitcase, praying he wouldn't drop her in the process.

"I'm going to scream," she warned. "My grandfather will shoot you."

"No, he won't. He's the one who said I'd need the handcuffs to make you listen."

She stilled. "He did not."

Spencer started down the hall. "Sure he did. His exact words were something on the order of you being as mad as a wet hen. But now he's probably ticked off at me because he told me to kidnap you quietly. He's reading."

He took advantage of her stillness to head for the stairs.

"When you set me down, Spencer Griffen, I'm going to pulverize you," she warned him calmly. "Then I'm going to strangle my grandfather."

"Fine. But first we talk."

"We can do that right here."

He found the front door standing open and silently blessed her grandfather. "My place."

"No."

"Yes. You're in no position to dictate terms here, lady." He carried her to his car, dropped the suitcase, and set her inside, panting heavily. "How come they always make this carrying bit look so easy on television?"

Brenna had stopped fighting him. Now she regarded him with an expression he couldn't decipher. "Why are you doing this?"

He leaned over to kiss the tip of her nose. "I plan to hold you hostage until you admit you love me."

Her lips parted. It took real restraint not to kiss them as well.

"You're insane," she breathed.

"No doubt." And he closed the door, carrying her suitcase to the trunk. Damn, but he loved this woman.

She didn't say a word as he reached over and buckled her seat belt. Not even when he accidentally brushed against her breast making both of them draw in a sharp breath.

"The plane had engine trouble," he told her, starting the car and backing down the driveway. "First we sat inside that cramped plane for two—count them—two solid hours. Do you know how loud an eighteen-month-old can scream? I swear to you the only reason they gave us another plane was because the kid was giving the repair crew a headache."

Brenna watched him silently. His words came faster as his nervousness grew.

"Then we waited for them to unloaded the baggage and transfer it to the other plane. The passengers were threatening mutiny at that point. I called you again, but there was still no answer."

She didn't say a word.

"We finally got to the skies over National Airport only to find planes stacked up everywhere, so we had to circle for what seemed like forever. The eighteen-month-old was not impressed with his twelfth view of the monuments. He was quite vocal on that point."

He shot her another look, but her expression still hadn't changed. Maybe the handcuffs had been a mistake.

"The fellow sitting next to me kept knotting his tie. I was afraid he was contemplating suicide by strangulation."

Brenna didn't crack a smile, but she did finally speak. "You didn't say anything about going out of town last night," she said quietly.

"I know. Once you told me you were wearing that nightgown, well, hell, you didn't expect any coherent conversation from me after that, did you?" He braked for a red light.

Brenna held up her hands. "Will you take these things off?"

"Eventually."

Her eyes narrowed. "Don't go getting kinky with me, Spencer."

"Hey, who's the one who wanted to rub my appendage with—"

"Never mind that! Where's the key?"

"What key?"

"To the handcuffs."

Spencer paused. "They didn't come with a key."

"You'd better be joking."

He turned into his parking lot and risked another glance at her face. "I'm serious. There is no key unless it was in the box my sister took."

She stared at him, apparently deciding he was telling the truth. "What am I going to do?"

"Don't worry. They're padded."

"Spencer—"

"Thank heavens you aren't wearing that gown I sent you. We'd get arrested going inside for sure. Although, I like the T-shirt. Sexy."

"It isn't supposed to be sexy, it's supposed to be comfortable."

"I've got news for you. It turns me on."

"Everything turns you on," she scoffed.

"Only when it relates to you."

He found a parking space right up front. "I'll carry you inside and come back for the bag."

"I'll walk."

He indicated her feet. "You don't have any shoes."

"Well, whose fault is that? Spencer, what are we going to do about these handcuffs?" She sounded genuinely nervous, this time.

"My plan is to chain you to my bed with them while I have my wicked way with you."

A sudden glimmer of answering excitement glinted in her eyes, only to fade beneath a fresh bout of anxiety.

"How are you going to get them open?"

Spencer reached over and pressed the hidden switch. The handcuff on her left hand sprang open.

"Oh."

"That's all you have to say?" He watched her changing expressions thinking he would never grow tired of looking at her. But underneath her bravado, he sensed she was still feeling vulnerable.

"I love you, Brenna."

The words settled in the silent car leaving him open and equally vulnerable. Spencer didn't breathe again until he saw the smile start in her eyes. It spread, creasing the area around her eyes before moving lower to tease the corners of her lips. And finally, her entire body seemed to swell with that smile. For the first time, Spencer felt certain that everything would be all right.

"I'll race you inside," she surprised him by saying.

She opened the door and Spencer started to chuckle. They were both laughing by the time they made it inside his apartment. He swept her into his arms and kissed her soundly. She molded against his body and he found she wasn't wearing a single thing under that T-shirt.

The loose handcuff smacked him in the side of the head, nearly dislodging his glasses when she threw her arms around his neck. Spencer lifted his head from her mouth and looked at her. She bubbled with excitement.

"Should we try for just a little bit kinky?" he asked. Her smile was incandescent. He led her into the bedroom and stripped the T-shirt from her body while her hands reached to push the sweater up and over his head.

"Lie down," he commanded.

"But you're still dressed."

"I know. And you're gloriously naked." He stroked her rounded buttock, easing her back onto the red satin sheets. "Raise your hands and slip them through the bars of the headboard."

Spencer watched her carefully for any sign of hesitation. Instead, anticipation bathed her in a rosy hue. When he reached for the loose handcuff, she allowed him to run the cuff through the bars behind her head. He clicked the metal around her other wrist and she quivered. Then he pulled back to stare at her, letting the delicious tension grow.

Brenna squirmed. "What are you doing?"

"Marvelling at how incredibly sexy you look, chained to my bed. I'm going to love every inch of your body—slowly." He bent and kissed the tip of one hard little nipple, pinching its companion lightly.

"Spencer! Take off your clothes."

"Soon." He feathered light kisses across her stomach, pausing to play with a yearning nipple, then palming the reactive planes of her stomach. The handcuffs clanged against the metal bars as she shifted beneath his tender assault. His palm hovered above the hair covering the apex of her thighs, lightly touching the crisp curls.

"I like seeing you all helpless like this," he told her.

"Just remember," she warned, "I get a turn next."

His erection strained at the material of his slacks. "I look forward to that."

He touched her, feeling the exciting dampness of her arousal. Spencer reveled at her skin's softness as his hand skimmed over her thigh and down her leg.

He added gentle kisses and tiny nips as he went, her body twisting in response. She made tiny sounds of pleasure that spurred him on. He paused to massage the soles of her feet, rubbing softly, watching her arch and stretch, wriggling helplessly against the cuffs.

"I want to touch you too," she said.

He kicked off his shoes and parted her legs. He wanted that too, but first, he wanted to bring her unprecedented pleasure.

"I know you do. That's part of the fun."

"Yes."

Her expression smoldered as Spencer kissed his way back up her leg.

"You're still dressed," she protested.

"I was trying to make this last," he said, "but that may not be possible." He unbuttoned his shirt, holding her gaze. "I think I'll keep you like this forever."

"You're really getting into this, aren't you?"

He grinned as he dropped his shirt to the floor. "Aren't you?"

She eyed the bulge in his pants. "Yes."

"Good."

"Touch me."

His hands paused at his belt buckle. "I need to get something first."

"What? Spencer, come back here!"

It only took a moment to grab the plastic jar from the kitchen. He twisted off the lid as he hurried back to the bedroom. "I still don't have any fruit, but how do you feel about peanut butter?"

Brenna tugged on the handcuffs. "You wouldn't dare."

He grinned and dipped his finger inside the container.

"You'll make a mess!" She squirmed, the handcuffs ringing against the metal.

"No, I won't." He dabbed a small amount of peanut butter on her navel. "I'm a very tidy eater." And he proceeded to show her exactly how neat he could be.

A long time later, with her snuggled against his shoulder, deeply asleep, Spencer realized he hadn't told her about his surprise. Oh well, after the incendiary loving they'd just completed, it might seem anticlimactic. Brenna loved him. She wasn't going anywhere. The news would keep until morning.

13

"SPENCER, GET UP!"

"Huh?"

Brenna shook him harder. "It's three minutes after twelve."

Spencer sat up in a rush. "It can't be."

Brenna tore her eyes from his chest and sternly forced her thoughts to behave. "Well, it is, and we have to be at Hadden's at one o'clock. I'm going to take a shower."

"I'll join you."

"No! We'll never get there if you join me."

"Party pooper."

She refused to smile, even if he was endearing. "Make yourself useful and go put some coffee on."

"Coffee. Gotcha. And may I say you look delectable this morning?"

"No, you may not. We don't have time." Brenna refused to let him see her blush, so she hurried into the bathroom.

Yesterday, she'd alternated between fear and a need to kill him. Then he stole into her room last night, and right back into her heart. No matter what he said, Spencer Griffen was a professional thief—he'd stolen her heart completely.

A week ago, she'd spent one entire evening composing reasons why a relationship between them couldn't last. Then he'd called her to ask her about her day in that slow, sexy voice of his, and she'd tossed the piece of paper in the trash.

She couldn't seem to stay mad at the man, even when her anger was justified. He needled her and bugged her until she saw the humor in the situation.

God help her, but she loved him. Totally, hopelessly, completely.

She finished her hasty shower and stepped out to dry her hair, only to find the man of her thoughts standing at the bathroom sink stark naked, a razor in one hand, lather in the other.

"What are you doing?" she asked.

"I'm shaving. Men do it every day. It's how we can kiss beautiful skin like yours without hurting it."

Brenna tried to look stern, but it was as impossible as keeping her eyes from moving down his body.

"Are you absolutely certain we have to be at Hadden's by one?" he asked.

"Yes," she said weakly. "Absolutely. What are you doing with that shaving cream?"

"Well, I just thought we might—"

"Spencer Griffen, don't you come near me."

"Maybe later?"

"Much later. Go take your shower."

"It would be more fun if we shared."

"Later."

She smiled as she pulled clothing from her suitcase. The crotchless panties fell from a handful. She looked at the bedroom door, heard the water running in the shower, and pulled on the panties. No one would know.

Except Spencer.

Later.

THEY WERE FASHIONABLY late and the house was filled with people. Brenna didn't see Kerry or Hadden at all, and it took them a while to find their grandparents.

"Nice of you to drop in," B. J. Wolford greeted.

"Benji, behave," Regina scolded.

Her grandfather stared at Brenna's hand, clasped firmly in Spencer's. Spencer refused to relinquish it, even when she tugged gently.

"Did you find the painting?" she asked.

"Nope. We started upstairs. Now we're working our way through the rooms down here," her grandfather told her.

"We'll join you," she said.

"I think we should start upstairs, too," Spencer said.

"But they've already looked up there."

"And maybe we'll see something they missed."

"But—"

"Run along," Regina urged. "We'll find you later."

"Why did you do that?" Brenna asked as Spencer pulled her toward the staircase.

"I want to talk to you."

"Oh." She thought of all the things she wanted to say to him as well, but this hardly seemed like the place or time.

Spencer began to wave.

"What are you doing?"

"Waving to Kerry."

Brenna spotted her friend's bright red hair in the crowd in the living room. She waved too, but Spencer was already tugging her up the stairs.

"You seem in an awfully big hurry."

"Not really. I just want to see that room in broad daylight."

"You mean you want to study the dirty pictures."

He used that naughty-boy smile that warned her to expect just about anything. "That too. I want to see which fruits work best where."

Brenna slapped his arm, but found she was a bit anxious to see Hadden's collection in the light as well. So were a lot of other people. The room was crowded.

Spencer stopped in front of what they'd come to call the fruit painting. "Hmm. Pineapples. I'm not overly fond of pineapples."

"Will you cut that out before someone hears?"

"Hey, they can make their own fruit salad. But it won't look as scrumptious as mine, or taste anywhere near as good." His gaze started all sorts of wicked sensations in her lower body.

She moved away from the painting and he followed. He stopped suddenly over by the desk and studied the scene by the waterfall. "Hmm. We're going to have to try the kitchen scene again. I don't think I had the position quite right."

"Spencer, I'm warning you..."

He kissed the top of her head, disarming her completely. "Okay, I'll behave," he lied.

"That would be a change."

"Let's go look in the bathroom again. We never did get much of a chance in there."

Before she could protest, he led her into the sybaritic bathroom. Another couple smiled and brushed past them, exiting into the bedroom. Quickly, Spencer closed the door and turned the lock.

"What are you doing?"

"This." And his mouth covered hers.

Brenna knew she should protest. And she would. Soon.

His hands roamed her body finally inching her skirt upward. Too late, Brenna remembered what she was wearing beneath the skirt.

When Spencer's hand reached her panties, his eyes widened in shock, then sparkled with excitement. "Why Brenna, you liked my present after all."

She was trying not to melt into a puddle. Trying to keep her wits in the face of an overwhelming need to repeat the wonders of the night before. "We can't do that here!"

He took her hand and pressed it over his erection.

"Want to bet?"

His lips closed over her protest. And someone pounded on the bathroom door.

"Griffen? You in there?"

"It's my grandfather!"

"Damn," Spencer muttered, releasing her.

He reached for the doorknob before she could protest. Her grandfather and Regina Griffen stood on the other side.

"Now, how did that door come to be locked?" Spencer asked innocently. "Have you seen this bathtub?"

Her grandfather frowned, but then his own excitement burst forth. "Never mind the bathtub. Come see what we found."

Brenna stepped forward, forgetting to be embarrassed. "You found the painting? You actually found it?"

"Come see for yourselves."

"Where is it? Do they know..." she lowered her voice and looked around, satisfied that no one else was paying them the least bit of attention "...the truth?"

"Benji's right, my dear. You really must come see it for yourself," Regina told her, glittering with excitement.

They followed the older couple down the staircase and into the dining room. Brenna suddenly realized they were being led toward the two B. J. Wolfords hanging on the far wall.

"There it is."

Her grandfather pointed to the still life.

"It's a bowl of fruit," Spencer said. He shared a half smile with Brenna and she knew he was thinking about the painting upstairs.

"That's right," her grandfather said. "It's a bowl of fruit. One of the earliest paintings I ever did."

"Doesn't look a thing like you, Grandma," Spencer teased.

"I don't understand," Brenna said in confusion.

Regina touched her hand. "Hadden had it restored. He had the nude removed and the painting below returned to its original state."

"You can do that?" Spencer asked.

Her grandfather nodded, his smile wide and free for the first time in a long time. "It's expensive as hell. And it doesn't always work. But Hadden had the money and knew all the right people. That's why you couldn't find the Lispkit. It doesn't exist anymore."

Brenna looked at Spencer and found him grinning. "I don't believe it," she said. "All that worry for nothing!"

"Oh, I wouldn't say it was for nothing." He drew her into his arms, ignoring their grandparents and anyone else who might care to watch. "I found you, didn't I? I love you, Brenna."

The truth of his words was clear. "I love you too," she managed to say.

"I know." He smiled gently.

"Egotist." But that smile stole her heart.

"I have a surprise for you," he said. "You know where I was yesterday?"

She shook her head.

"New York. I had a job interview with Racer Engineering. They offered me a job at a fantastic salary and I said yes."

Brenna pulled free. "You aren't serious."

"Of course I'm serious."

"Turn it down!"

"What's the matter with you? I thought you'd be pleased."

"Pleased? Pleased? You can't give up your job. I just gave up mine! I got my old boss to offer me another position here in D.C. I start in two weeks."

Brenna heard her grandfather start to snicker. Regina shushed him, but Spencer didn't even glance at the two.

"Tell them you changed your mind," he insisted.

"I can't tell them that! You'll just have to tell Racer you changed *your* mind."

"But, it's a good job, Brenna."

She jammed a finger against his chest. "Listen, buster, your career is just as important as mine, and I say we live here. You're in line to make partner here."

"I know that, but the Racer outfit is offering me a hell of a raise. Just tell your people you changed your mind."

"Who put you in charge?"

"I can see the wedding now," B. J. Wolford told Regina Griffen, taking her hand and leading her away. "The minister will have to use a fire hose to separate them at the altar, and they'll probably start a food fight at the reception."

"At least it won't be dull," Regina agreed. "And just look at what spirited great-grandchildren we should get from this match. I do think we should go find young Hadden and buy your painting back, Benji."

"Good idea. We'll give it to the two of them for a wedding gift—if they don't kill each other first."

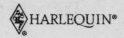

Not The Same Old Story!

Exciting, glamorous romance stories that take readers around the world.

Sparkling, fresh and tender love stories that bring you pure romance.

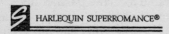
Bold and adventurous— Temptation is strong women, bad boys, great sex!

Provocative and realistic stories that celebrate life and love.

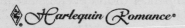
Contemporary fairy tales—where anything is possible and where dreams come true.

Heart-stopping, suspenseful adventures that combine the best of romance and mystery.

Humorous and romantic stories that capture the lighter side of love.

Take 2 bestselling love stories FREE

Plus get a FREE surprise gift!

Special Limited-Time Offer

Mail to Harlequin Reader Service®

> 3010 Walden Avenue
> P.O. Box 1867
> Buffalo, N.Y. 14240-1867

YES! Please send me 2 free Harlequin Temptation® novels and my free surprise gift. Then send me 4 brand-new novels every month, which I will receive before they appear in bookstores. Bill me at the low price of $3.12 each plus 25¢ delivery and applicable sales tax, if any.* That's the complete price, and a saving of over 10% off the cover prices—quite a bargain! I understand that accepting the books and gift places me under no obligation ever to buy any books. I can always return a shipment and cancel at any time. Even if I never buy another book from Harlequin, the 2 free books and the surprise gift are mine to keep forever.

142 HEN CH7G

Name	(PLEASE PRINT)
Address	Apt. No.
City	State	Zip

This offer is limited to one order per household and not valid to present Harlequin Temptation® subscribers. *Terms and prices are subject to change without notice. Sales tax applicable in N.Y.

UTEMP-98

©1990 Harlequin Enterprises Limited

Presents Extravaganza

25 YEARS!

It's our birthday
and we're celebrating....

Twenty-five years of romance fiction
featuring men of the world and captivating women—
Seduction and passion guaranteed!

Not only are we promising you three months of terrific
books, authors and romance, but as an added **bonus**
with the retail purchase of two Presents® titles,
you can receive a special one-of-a-kind keepsake.
It's our gift to you!

Look in the back pages of any Harlequin Presents® title,
from May to July 1998, for more details.

Available wherever Harlequin books are sold.

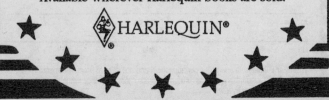

HARLEQUIN®

Heat up your summer this July with

Summer Lovers

This July, bestselling authors Barbara Delinsky,
Elizabeth Lowell and Anne Stuart present three
couples with pasts that threaten their future happiness.
Can they play with fire without being burned?

FIRST, BEST AND ONLY
by Barbara Delinsky

GRANITE MAN
by Elizabeth Lowell

CHAIN OF LOVE
by Anne Stuart

Available wherever Harlequin and Silhouette books
are sold.

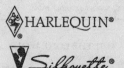

HARLEQUIN®

Silhouette®

Look us up on-line at: http://www.romance.net   HREQ798

COMING NEXT MONTH

#693 1-800-HERO JoAnn Ross
Hero for Hire

When Lucas Kincaid agreed to guard the *very* delectable body of writer Grace Fairfield, he had no idea what lay in store. Someone wanted the beautiful Grace dead, and the list of suspects was long. But his biggest challenge was making the woman who wrote about happy endings believe that Lucas could be the man for her.

#694 THE PRINCESS AND THE P.I. Donna Sterling

Billionaire heiress Claire Richmond had run away to sow some wild oats, only to realize she wasn't equipped to deal with the "real" world. Luckily, her cousin sent a detective after her. With strong and sexy Tyce Walker by her side, Claire had no fear...which only proved to Tyce what a complete innocent she was, and what a rat *he* was.

#695 SINGLE IN THE SADDLE Vicki Lewis Thompson
Mail Order Men

Daphne Proctor used *Texas Men* magazine to find a husband—and it worked! She was already half in love with cowboy Stony Arnett just through his letters. But nothing had prepared her for the overwhelming chemistry that sizzled between them in person. It seemed like fate. Until Daphne discovered Stony *hadn't* placed the ad—and that he had no use for a wife....

#696 SUMMER HEAT Pamela Burford and Patricia Ryan

Sand and surf, romantic sunsets, a house on the beach...and a sexy stranger to share it all with. What more could you ask from a vacation? In *July*, uptight Quinn could have lived without mellow Molly, who showered naked outside and stayed up all night.... In *August*, Tom wished Sally wanted him for more than just a passionate holiday fling, though if that's all he could have.... *Two steamy novels from two hot authors, together in one very special summer read!*

AVAILABLE NOW:

#689 BLACK VELVET
Carrie Alexander

#690 THE NAKED TRUTH
Dani Sinclair

#691 THE LONE WOLF
Sandy Steen

#692 THE WRONG MAN IN WYOMING
Kristine Rolofson